CROCODILE LEGION

by S.J.A. Turney,

illustrated by Dave Slaney

Published in this format 2016 by Mulcahy Books

Cover design by Dave Slaney

First Edition

ISBN: 978-0-9935552-3-7

For Marcus and Callie - always adventurous, never dull.

And for Midge and Jim, Dave's mum and dad, the latter sadly no longer with us, but looking down from a billion stars. Love you forever, Dave. x

Dave would like to thank his wife Lisa and son Jake - for putting up with him, and Simon would like to thank his wife Tracey for her patience and periodic feeding with pies. Dave and Simon would like to thank the generous Robin Carter for introducing us in the first place, and the talented Sallyanne at Mulcahy Associates for all her hard work and genius in turning our wacky scribblings into a great book.

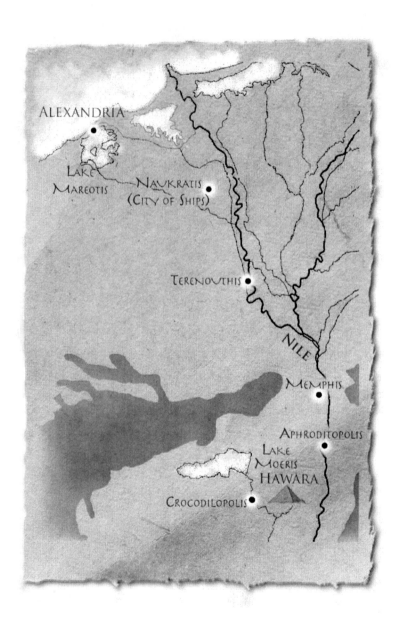

ALEXANDRIA

LAKE
MAREOTIS

NAUKRATIS
(CITY OF SHIPS)

TERENOUTHIS

NILE

MEMPHIS

APHRODITOPOLIS

LAKE
MOERIS
HAWARA

CROCODILOPOLIS

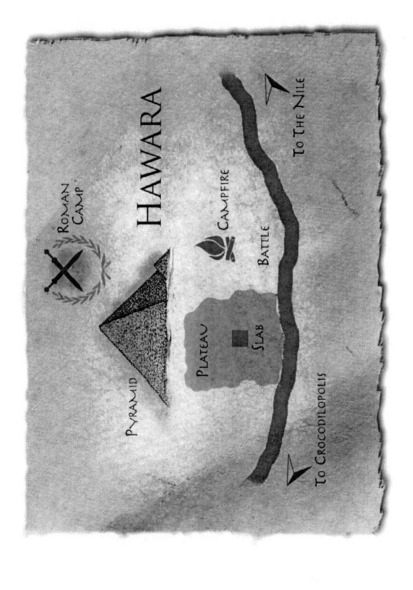

PROLOGUE

Egypt, 117AD

There was a clang as something glinting and worth more than a year's pay hit the floor and rolled off into a corner.

'Inkaef!'

'What?'

A figure, tanned by the blazing Egyptian sun and dressed in a simple white skirt, turned in the darkness of the chamber, his torch held high.

'Do we take the coffin?'

'We take *everything*, Pashedu.'

The second figure, dressed much the same as the first, nodded in the darkness of the chamber, lit only by the flickering orange glow of three torches and the dancing reflections of that light on the gold and the gems that filled the room like the richest treasury on Earth.

'I don't want to touch the mummy, Inkaef. How can I take the coffin from around it without touching it?'

The white-skirted leader rolled his eyes, unseen in the gloom. 'You could grow up, stop acting like a frightened baby and just *do it!*'

Inkaef bent back to the collection of small gold and ebony wood idols of the gods and stuffed them into the sack he held, which was already weighed down with loot.

'What if we get caught?' came another voice from near the mummy's coffin.

'Who by?' snapped Inkaef. 'We're not going to get caught. Just get that coffin free and carry it outside. It's made of enough gold to buy a small town.'

'Oh, no. Oh, *poop*!' came yet another voice from the ante-chamber.

'What is it?' asked Inkaef irritably, ducking in through the door, where he saw one of the other men cowering, backing towards him.

'It's *alive*, Inkaef! It's coming to eat me for what we've done!'`

Inkaef held up his torch to see what it was his companion was backing away from. A tall statue with one leg stretched forward as if to walk loomed in the dark corner of the room. The statue's body was dusty and brown in its pleated white skirt, but its head was that of Sobek the crocodile god, all jagged white teeth and green scaly flesh and yellow, slitted eyes. He had to admit that it gave even *him* a moment of fright.

'It's a *statue*, Temun. Nothing more frightening than a statue. Now load the loot and start moving things out.'

He smiled up at the crocodile face looming in the gloom.

'But you… you give me ideas…'

CHAPTER 1

Marcus scratched his unmanageable brown hair and watched Centurion Gallo swing his heavy sword, chopping pieces from the wooden post in the training yard as the relentless Egyptian sun beat down upon him. The centurion glistened with sweat and had to be suffering an urgent thirst for the jug of water which sat between Marcus and his sister Callie beneath the veranda a few paces away, for his eyes kept straying to it. All around the square the legionaries of the century – eighty men trained to be the best in the Roman army – mirrored their centurion's actions, cutting lumps from innocent wooden posts, imagining them to be giant, hairy barbarians threatening the peace of the empire, just as Marcus did in his mind's eye.

He imagined himself older and bulkier, swinging his sword as a great big German ran at him screaming a horrible war cry. One day it would be him, when he was old enough for the legions. He watched the exercise in the yard and swept his own rough-hewn wooden sword back and forth, raising puffs of dust into the sizzling air.

'I don't know why you bother, Marcus. They'll never let *you* fight. You're too small and pale and skinny. *And* you're frightened of heights!'

Marcus flashed an irritated glance at his sister, who was grinning her most mischievous grin in the dazzling sunshine, her white-gold hair almost blinding in the light. 'I'm ten!' Marcus snapped. 'Another four years and I'll be old enough to apply to the legion. And *Gallo* says I can try at twelve, anyway,' he added smugly. 'That's only *two* years, so I want to be ready.'

Callie took a sip of her drink and kicked her sandaled heels against the stonework at the edge of the training square as she scribbled the latest entry in her journal on the expensive vellum sheet. Marcus sighed. There was no arguing with his sister – although arguing was certainly one of her favourite pastimes, so his refusal to accept her opinion was generally no reason for her to stop. Yet today she seemed a little distracted and let the subject drop with uncharacteristic ease.

Marcus had been set on joining the legion ever since they had lost their parents – three years it had now been since ma and pa disappeared at sea on the journey to Crete. It had been a hard time for both of them, but really they had been very lucky. Most children in their position would have ended up begging on the streets of Alexandria, but Marcus and Callie had been saved from such a fate. Their uncle, Gaius Scriptor, was a standard bearer in the 22nd legion based in that same city, and he had, with only a little argument from his commanders, taken Marcus and Callie in.

Children and family were forbidden to serving soldiers by law, but adopted nephews and nieces seemed to somehow be exempt from the rules, and even the legion's senior officers had seen to it that they had a roof over their head and three meals a day. Of course, they *worked* for it. Marcus ran messages and carried out small jobs for the soldiers in return for his room and board and a few coins each payday, and Callie, already an advanced reader at eight years of age, had a better grasp of writing than many of the soldiers and spent much of her time aiding Potens, the engineer, with his plans. And when Potens didn't need her, the others could always find easy jobs for her pen... when they could pin the elusive little sprite down long enough, anyway.

It had been a blessing for them both. Life with the legionaries had filled their time and helped them deal with the loss of their parents, and over the last three years their uncle's entire century of men had adopted the pair, treating them like members of the unit.

The sounds of legionaries thumping wooden posts failed to drown out the regular scratching sounds of the pen on the vellum and the noises of dipping for fresh ink. Almost all Callie's chore money went on writing materials. Her journal had begun the day they had heard about mum and dad, and had been kept religiously ever since. Early on, she had jealously guarded its contents as private and Marcus had tried time after time to sneak a peek at the writings. Then, one winter night, he had managed to spend a few minutes peering at them and had immediately wished he had not, since the bulk of the early pages he had seen had been about their parents. Since then he had given her the privacy she'd demanded.

Marcus swung his wooden sword absently, watching his little sister. Though she was ever cheeky and sprightly, sometimes he stole a glance at her when she thought no one was looking, and there would be a sad little wobble to her lip. He resolved to stop fighting with her so often. After all, the last thing he had ever told his parents was that he would look after her while they were away.

'I see you're having fun, sir,' laughed a light voice from behind, and the two children spun with a smile to see their uncle approaching. The centurion ripped his sword from the post where it had become temporarily stuck and turned, wiping the sweat from his heavy brow with a hand like a joint of ham.

Uncle Scriptor stood smiling with his arms folded beneath the shade of the sloping roof. Tall and lean, he had a cool, refreshed look despite the heat, and Gallo grumbled about some people not working hard enough to break a sweat.

'Uncle,' squealed Callie and scrambled to her feet, running off to hug the tall man. Marcus just nodded and took a few more practice swings with his wooden blade.

'Don't you two have anything to do?'

'No,' grinned Callie. 'I just finished the new aqueduct listings with Potens.'

'And I'm training,' breathed Marcus, lunging out with the sword.

Scriptor smiled, patted Callie on her head, and strode to the edge of the courtyard where he gestured to the century's commander as he bent, picked up Marcus' wooden cup from the veranda floor, and took an appreciative swig of the cold fruit drink. 'You don't have to train with the men, sir. There's no one in the century who can swing a sword like you.'

Marcus gave his uncle a sour look at the comment and redoubled his effort with *his* weapon. One day *he* would be the best...

'And do you know why I'm good?' Gallo grumbled, wiping away more sweat. 'Because I keep practicing, like your nephew there. Not swanning around in the shade and drinking chilled pomegranate juice like *some* I could mention. A fine example to set for a lad who's only a few years from joining us!'

As Marcus' heart leapt to hear the centurion say such a thing, Uncle Scriptor laughed carelessly. He was the only man in the century who could get away with chuckling at the centurion's moods because Gallo knew as well as anyone that despite his clean, well-dressed and sweat-free appearance, the standard bearer was as good a swordsman as any of them... better than most, in fact.

'Pomegranate juice is good for you, sir,' the standard bearer chuckled, swigging from Marcus' wooden cup again before putting it back on the step. 'Makes you fart too,' he laughed, ripping out a thunderous rumble close enough to Marcus' head that he took a few swift paces along the veranda to be out of the smelly cloud. 'And we're lucky we're based here on the north coast,' their uncle added, 'where the river delta is so wide and all the fruit grows. Imagine being stationed in the south, where it's all red desert and dusty rocks? A whole year could pass where the only time you'd ever see a pomegranate is in your dreams, sir.'

Gallo nodded fervently, and Marcus could quite understand why. He'd talked to enough of the veterans to know that any soldier stationed in Alexandria thanked the gods almost every day that he was based here by the cool sea and not in the dry, hot south, where the desert people lived and water was scarce.

'Anyway,' the centurion griped, 'now that you've interrupted me and I've lost my rhythm, what did you want?'

Uncle Scriptor scratched his smooth chin and gave a lop-sided smile.

'You've been called to the prefect's office.'

Marcus blinked. The *prefect*?

Even Callie scurried forward again to the step, her interest piqued. The prefect was the most powerful man in Egypt – the Roman governor of this ancient land, appointed directly by the emperor. He rarely saw soldiers or civilians except of the highest rank, yet the centurion had been summoned to his office. And it sounded as though their uncle was going too. Marcus held his breath, tense. The prefect controlled Egypt and its army. There was nothing he couldn't do.

Please don't make me stay behind, he thought.

He saw Gallo's frown as the centurion wiped his gleaming blade on the rag tucked into his belt and slid it into his scabbard. Clearly Gallo was surprised at the summons too.

'You'd better clean yourself up, sir,' their uncle said to his superior, 'and get dressed in your armour. You smell like a hippopotamus after a long wallow in the mud.'

'That's probably your wind, uncle,' grinned Callie, earning a disapproving frown from Marcus. That was no way to speak to an important standard bearer, even if he was your uncle.

11

Scriptor, however, simply smiled at her and stroked her gleaming blond hair – a trait so rare in Egypt that she was more or less unique in the city.

The centurion was shaking his head – he had met prefect Turbo a few times. 'Unlike his amiable and quiet predecessor, *this* governor seems to be a man who would appreciate a soldier for what he is, and not for the gleam of his breastplate. I'm fine as I am.'

Leaving the men chopping pieces out of the numerous wooden posts, Gallo wiped his perspiring face on the same rag from his belt and then threw it down with the pile of clothes and armour that Marcus had been guarding on the veranda. With a stretch, he walked from the training ground and into the shade of the headquarters complex at the centre of the fortress.

Marcus threw a hopeful look at his uncle, and Scriptor pursed his lips and frowned for a moment before giving him a nod and a smile and turning to follow the centurion. The two children shared a happy grin and Marcus sheathed his wooden sword in his belt as the pair made to follow the two officers, but the standard bearer paused for a moment and arched his eyebrows at them.

'Uncle?'

Scriptor pointed behind them and with a guilty look, Marcus and Callie hurried back and collected the centurion's leather tunic, chainmail shirt and scarf, hurrying to catch up and struggling to carry the heavy weight between them.

This army base which stood on the north coast of Egypt overlooking the clear blue waters of the Mediterranean Sea was a massive place, home to two full Roman legions and their officers as well as a few lucky hangers-on like Marcus and Callie. But more than that, since the revolts and civil unrest of the recent years had left much of the city of Alexandria in ruins, the prefect had moved his offices and all his staff from the old city's palace into the army's fortress, meaning that the place was now the centre of both military and civil power in Egypt. An exciting place for a childhood, whether you were a would be legionary like Marcus or an academic scamp like Callie.

Between painted columns and through the huge marble hall with its enormous statues of Mars and the emperor they scurried in the wake of their uncle and his centurion. Marcus' eyes played briefly across the statues. The emperor's one was new, just like the emperor himself. The clean-shaven war hero and man of the people, Trajan, had passed away last month and his successor, Hadrian, now stood bearded and fresh beside Mars the war god. *So new*, in fact that the bright paint that made the statue realistic had not yet begun to fade.

Marcus drank in every ounce of detail as they passed through the headquarters. He had been in the place a few times on errands for the soldiers, but it never ceased to impress him. From this great sprawling complex not only two legions, but the whole of Egypt was run. One day – perhaps soon, if the prefect were to notice an eager young recruit with a practice sword at his side – Marcus would stand before that great statue of Mars and take his oath to the legions.

The prefect's office was a small room off the side of the big hall, close to the shrines where the legions' flags and eagles were kept, and two legionaries stood on guard outside his door. Both of them looked hard at the approaching soldiers and the children at their heels, trying to decide whether a sweaty man in a dirty tunic and two meddlesome brats should be sent away immediately. The sight of Scriptor among them, however, made it clear that they were officers, despite the state of the centurion. The legionaries snapped to attention and saluted as the four approached.

'Centurion Gallo here to see the prefect.'

Marcus watched the legionaries share a surprised look, then nod to Gallo and step aside so that they could enter. He bit his lip nervously as the two soldiers gave him and Callie a hard look, and their uncle bent low and hissed at them. 'Stay at the back, say nothing, and look useful.'

14

They were to be allowed in! Marcus had hardly dared to hope, assuming they would be made to wait outside in the great hall. His heart soaring, he nodded, Callie beside him looking a little preoccupied as she struggled to open her wax writing tablet while holding the centurion's big heavy leather tunic. They were going to be in the office of the province's governor – a man basically all-powerful in Egypt. A man who could even waive any age requirement for the legion if he wished. Marcus struggled with the centurion's armour, trying to neaten his unruly hair in order to make the best impression he could.

Inside the office, Turbo – the prefect of Egypt – sat at his desk with lists and letters and maps arrayed before him. He looked up at Gallo and with one glance Marcus knew that the centurion had made the right decision in not changing into his smart uniform. Far from disapproval at the officer's rough state, Turbo simply nodded and pointed to the seat opposite as he worked on his list, his gaze passing across the standard bearer and the two children with barely a frown.

Marcus felt himself flush, and tried to force the warmth in his face to fade. He needed to look capable. Like a grown man. He turned very slightly so that the worn wooden sword at his side would be visible, struggling with his burden. It was faintly irritating that Callie looked so calm and comfortable, but then his sister had nothing to lose here. *She* didn't have to look ready to be a legionary.

Centurion Gallo cleared his throat to ask a question, but the prefect held up a finger, indicating that he should wait, and pointed at the seat again.

The centurion sat. Behind him, Scriptor stood at perfect attention while Marcus at the back gritted his teeth and tried not to acknowledge the shaking of his arms bearing the heavy weight of the chainmail. He was just wondering if dropping armour on the prefect's lovely mosaic floor would constitute a beating offence when, with a grin, Callie dumped the leather tunic she'd been carrying on top of her brother's burden and pulled out her pen to write on her tablet, the tip of her tongue protruding from the corner of her mouth as she worked. Marcus let out a little grunt and changed his stance to bear the weight better, flashing his sister an angry look before gazing up at the ruler of Egypt before him.

Prefect Turbo reminded him of one of the scraggy black vultures that they often saw circling in the clear blue Egyptian skies. The most powerful man in the province sat hunched over his desk, his neck craned and his head snapping back and forth as he worked. Finally, he straightened and looked at the man in the seat opposite him.

'Gallo? Good. Your legion's commander tells me that you are a centurion who gets the job done quickly and efficiently?'

The centurion nodded and Marcus felt his pulse quicken. This sounded exciting and important, and happily he hadn't been excluded from the meeting.

'Your man here and your slaves are to be trusted?'

Marcus felt a wave of embarrassment and dismay wash over him at the realisation that the prefect thought they were the centurion's slaves. He felt the flush rising in his cheeks again and his lip wobble slightly. Callie shut her tablet with a loud *snap*, bridling, and Marcus could see she was about to complain about being labelled a slave. With a quick sidestep and juggling his heavy load, he clapped his hand over her mouth to keep her quiet. She turned irritably to argue, but their uncle cast a warning look at them both and they subsided quickly, glaring at each other before turning back to the prefect.

Ignoring the exchange, the centurion nodded. 'This is my standard bearer and his wards.'

Prefect Turbo replaced his list among the others on the table, stood and strode across to a large map of Egypt hanging on the wall. Marcus tried to focus on the map's details, despite the enormous strain the pile of gear was putting on him. The prefect's finger tapped the chart at the rough position of

Alexandria, the battered city a few minutes' walk from the fortress gate. Once one of the greatest cities in the world, it currently languished in ruins in the aftermath of a war.

'Alexandria is a mess, centurion.'

'Yes sir.'

'My predecessor did an excellent job of stopping the revolt, but he left the city ruined and the treasury worryingly empty in the process. The new emperor expects me to have Alexandria back to its thriving best within the year, and he is not a man to accept failure lightly.'

Again, Gallo nodded without comment, but Marcus' forehead creased into a frown – he could see several problems with the idea of rebuilding the city. Only a third of the place still stood intact. Most buildings had been damaged – burned or destroyed in the riots – and trade was slower than a one-legged dog in a strong wind. The ports that were usually full of ships from all over the world – including the fated one that had taken their parents away three years ago – were often empty these days, with traders even from nearby Crete only docking once every few weeks. No gladiatorial games or chariot races had been staged since the revolt. Even the nobles were feeling the pinch of poverty in their purses now, let alone the common folk who carried on the farming and trade that built Egypt's wealth.

'You see my problem?' the prefect mused.

'It is an impossible task, sir.'

Marcus nodded his silent agreement in the background, hurriedly grabbing the leather tunic as it started to slide from his armful. Callie hung her tablet from her belt, produced a bag of dates from somewhere and began to chew on one noisily, earning another sharp glance from their uncle which she blithely ignored. Marcus glared at her, but she paid no more attention to him than she did to their uncle.

'It *is* impossible with no money in the treasury,' conceded the prefect. 'Back in Rome, I was led to believe that Egypt was rich. For thousands of years it has been the land of grain and of gold. And yet I arrive here to find its biggest city needs rebuilding and not even a few coins in the coffers, let alone those legendary tons of gold.'

Marcus stood quietly, hoping his arms would survive the interview – the strain was becoming almost unbearable. He had a feeling he knew where this was going, and from Gallo's expression, so did he.

'I need gold, centurion,' the prefect said, slapping the palms of his hands down on the table and confirming Marcus' suspicion. 'I have asked my advisors how it can be done, and they can suggest only one source.'

'Sir?'

'The *pharaohs* who used to rule Egypt were as wealthy as gods and were buried with mountains of gold. I am told that robbing their pyramids has become something of a national sport over the centuries. Well now their contents can help me rebuild Alexandria for the emperor instead of lining the pockets of thieves.'

Marcus felt a chill run down his spine. *Tomb robbing*? The men of the two legions of Alexandria were used to being sent to *prevent* the tombs of the ancient kings being raided. Now this new prefect would have the soldiers do it themselves? There would be trouble. Marcus could barely imagine the danger and the unpopularity the soldiers might suffer if they robbed a pharaoh's tomb. His gaze slid to his sister, whose eyes had widened and were sparkling. Typical! He rolled his own eyes and then paid attention as he realised centurion Gallo was talking again.

'Sir, most of the pyramids and tombs have already been robbed long ago... all the ones in the north near us, certainly. The nearest ones that are still intact will be more than a hundred miles south in the desert.'

There didn't seem much chance that the fact would deter the prefect, but it was the truth, nevertheless. Marcus realised he was holding his breath and forced himself to exhale, his arms still quivering with the weight of the centurion's gear.

Turbo narrowed his eyes.

'They told me you were a man who could get the job done? The *job* is to refill the treasury so that I can rebuild the emperor's city. They tell me that pyramids are filled with gold. They tell me that not all of them have been robbed. You will find one of those, centurion, and you will empty it for me.'

Gallo sighed but nodded his agreement and Marcus felt a thrill of frightened excitement. 'Yes sir,' the centurion replied. 'It might take a few weeks, though, sir. We will have to travel a long way. And we first have to learn where there *is* such a place, which could be a monumental task in itself.'

The prefect frowned, drummed his fingers on the map for a moment longer, and then returned to his seat.

'I understand that Alexandria is home to the world's greatest library?'

'Some of it, sir. Much of it has gone'

Marcus nodded, thinking back to the stories that Callie had read him from the histories. When he was in the city visiting Cleopatra, the great Julius Caesar had accidentally burned down most of the library.

'Yes, well…' the prefect sighed, 'use what is left. There must be some information there.'

'Yes sir.'

There was a moment of silence and Turbo returned to his 'vulture hunch' over the table, studying his lists. After a while he looked up.

'You still here?'

'Sir?'

'Go and find me a pharaoh's gold, centurion. Dismissed.'

Gallo stood, saluted, and plodded from the room with Scriptor close at his heel. Callie trotted off after them, selecting another date from the bag and sucking at it noisily. Marcus turned as best he could, his blood running cold as he felt his arm give way and the mail shirt slip to the delicate mosaic floor with a noise like a thousand nails landing in a marble bath. He looked up in horror to see prefect Turbo gazing at him, one eyebrow arched meaningfully. Feeling any chance of early admittance into the legion slip away, Marcus flushed bright red and stooped, collecting up the mail shirt, bowing his head awkwardly and staggering from the room after the rest of them.

The guards outside the door grinned at Marcus' beet-red face as he passed to find his uncle and Gallo standing in the great hallway, admiring the statue of the new emperor while Callie excavated a tooth with a frown of concentration.

'First emperor to wear a beard,' the standard bearer smiled to his centurion as Marcus came to a halt behind them. 'They say he does it to hide scars on his chin, but I'll bet you a week's pay every officer in the army starts to grow a beard now, just to be like him. I reckon it's been a few days since even the prefect shaved.'

Gallo grumbled miserably. 'No one in their right mind would want a beard when they live in Egypt. This place is hot enough when you're nearly bald!'

As Marcus stood, red-faced and sweating, Uncle Scriptor turned his grin on the centurion. 'What do we do now, then, sir?'

'We are to become tomb robbers, Scriptor. The new prefect wants a pharaoh's gold to help him rebuild the city and, just like the emperor, he's not the sort to accept failure, so we'll find an untouched pyramid and take all its treasure for him. Simple as that.'

Marcus felt that same tension again as he held his breath. There was nothing he wanted more than to join the century on their mission, but there was very little chance the officers would want to take two children with them – especially a young girl. And he couldn't imagine going *without* Callie, even if it meant moving one step closer to enlistment. He had promised to protect her. He could feel himself trembling with apprehension.

'Tomb robbing, though, sir? The lads aren't going to like that.'

'I cannot say I'm a huge fan myself, Scriptor, but we are soldiers, and soldiers follow orders.'

'So what are *your* orders, sir?'

'We are off to the city to track down an untouched pyramid, Scriptor. Find Senex and just the three of us will go. No need to interrupt the rest of the men's training.' Marcus let out a small gasp of disappointment at being excluded and for the first time since they'd entered the building, the centurion seemed to notice the two children. 'Best bring them too. Might be a lot of scrolls to check and carry.'

Callie produced the stray piece of date from her mouth with a flourish, and Marcus grinned with pleasure. They were going to help plan the expedition. The centurion *needed* them!

CHAPTER 2

Callie's journal

We are going to do something that takes us out of the fortress. The prefect himself has given Uncle's unit the job of hunting down an unrobbed pharaoh's pyramid and taking all its gold for the rebuilding of Alexandria. Marcus seems to think we will be going along and that he is almost a soldier in the legion now. He might be right – about us going, not about him being a soldier. He is lucky, though, even if he's not a soldier, and both uncle and Potens know I'm clever. I do not want to stay behind in Alexandria, neither on my own, nor with Marcus. Where Uncle Scriptor goes, we go. I will have it no other way.

Marcus will persuade Uncle, but I will make myself indispensable. As Hannibal said about crossing the Alps: 'Aut viam inveniam aut faciam' – I will either find a way or I will make one. Old Senex will know all about the local religions, but the history of this place and its language are obscure. I will secure us a place with this journey one way or another, and we will help to find the gold and bring it back. Though I dislike the idea of robbing a tomb, the living folk of Alexandria are in desperate need, and the gold would change everything.

And if we do well, and Prefect Turbo is pleased with us, then possibly he might help me with my own quest. After all, he rules Egypt.

He can approve anything.

Alexandria was a depressing sight and the three soldiers, now fully armoured and attired in red dress uniform, kept their eyes ahead as they marched along the neatly paved roads between the city's wreckage. Callie bounced along behind them, seemingly oblivious to the ruination all about, but Marcus was focused and excited, relieved of his burden now and ready to help.

The enormous Jewish quarter – through which they passed and which covered the entire eastern end of the city – was where the riots had started and where most of the action had taken place in the revolt. It was now little more than a collection of ruins and rubble and jagged walls jutting up to the clear sky like crumbled brown fangs and Marcus found himself picturing the spires as the home of wicked Titans and imagined himself swinging a sword at them. He had to force himself to stop daydreaming and pay attention. If he was to be a soldier one day then he had to learn to focus on the job at hand, even if it involved a tiring trek through ruined streets filled with homeless beggars.

Passing across the narrow bridge over the canal, the small party marched along the edge of the harbour of Lake Mareotis, past the crumbling monumental city centre and into the western district, where the damage had been less thorough. As they passed the end of the street which had once held the children's

27

home – now a broken wreck like so many others – Marcus turned a sad face away from it, but Callie peered down with interest, unperturbed. And then they were past and nearing their goal.

Once upon a time, the great library of Alexandria had been the envy of the world – the greatest collection of books and scrolls in existence. Then, a hundred and fifty years ago, the great Julius Caesar had started a fire which had burned much of the city, including the main branch of the library. Luckily for book-lovers everywhere, the library's overflow was kept in the great temple of Serapis on the far side of town, and consequently had survived the blaze.

Now, as the five of them passed through the streets, Marcus forced himself to ignore the pleading arms of those poor souls who had lost their homes in the riots, and to concentrate on their objective: the great *Serapeum* temple that rose outside the walls on a rocky bump which gave it a commanding position. The party paused for a moment to let Callie catch up, the girl having dropped to the roadside with a sympathetic smile to give the rest of her bag of dates to a desperate and hungry little wretch. Marcus smiled at her. Flighty she may be, but she would never be uncaring. His sister fell in line next to him with a saddened face.

'You can't help them all, you know.'

Callie nodded unhappily. 'I shouldn't have to. Why are there wars?'

Marcus sighed. His sister was well versed in history and he knew that she could answer that herself, but somehow, seeing the hopelessness of the beggars had cracked the shell of her optimism and made her sad. Though she'd not said it, he could see in her eyes that somehow the orphaned girl she had helped had brought back memories of their own parents.

'There will always be wars, Callie. But the legions are not here to start them. Uncle and his friends are there to put a stop to things like the riots that ruined the city. That's why I want to be in them, like dad was before he met mum.'

He immediately regretted saying that as a tear leaked from his sister's eye and he hugged her tight, releasing her only as they had to scurry to catch up. 'Don't be sad. You're going to the great library. More books than you could ever hope to read!'

Callie smiled quietly, grateful for her brother's timely changing of the subject. 'And you never know, Marcus,' she replied with something of her customary zeal, 'you might get to go on the expedition yourself.'

'Not without you, sis,' he smiled. 'Not without you.'

The whitewashed walls and red tiled roofs of the enormous temple stood out against the repetitive golden brown local stone of the landscape and the poorer buildings. This temple to the healing bull-god of the Egyptians contained only a fraction of the former great library, yet remained one of the greatest collections in the world regardless.

Crowning the rise outside the walls, the Serapeum was surrounded by low-grade warehousing which was mostly empty and silent since the revolt.

Uncle Scriptor, who lugged the century's heavy standard around, was also the man who kept the century's records and read out letters to those men who didn't know how to read or write, but his ability with words was easily outstripped by his niece. Callie's command of language and voracious appetite for books were famous among the century – the girl who read every book that came her way, and absorbed information the way a sponge absorbs water.

Thus in her few moments of idle time she had occasionally crossed the city in the company of her engineer friend, Potens, and spent time in the library of the Serapeum, filling her head with dusty facts and figures for which Marcus could see little use. Now, he could almost feel his sister buzzing beside him with the excitement of the library being so close, her earlier sadness all but forgotten.

By contrast, Senex – who walked ahead with the centurion and was the oldest man in the unit – only read what directly affected him, and often asked others even to read that to him, since his eyes pained him when he had to concentrate too hard. Senex was in charge of all the century's religious duties. It was said he'd been a trainee priest all those years ago before he'd joined the army, and he knew magic tricks, too. Marcus liked him for those tricks and for the fact that the old man tended to include him in the unit's religious ceremonies, and Senex grinned at the pair with his few remaining teeth as they neared the great temple.

The five of them left the broken city gate and approached the steps of the Serapeum, sidestepping a line of carts that rolled along the street, the oxen pulling them unaware that they should be moving out of the way of officers. Gallo harrumphed with irritation as he had to move around the smelly beasts and Marcus spared a brief glance as the carts pulled up outside a warehouse opposite and native workers scrambled all over them.

Apparently deciding that the mission was too important for distractions and letting the workers and their burdens off with just a glare, the centurion led his men and the two children up the steps and into the temple. Inside, an attendant priest asked what they required and, when Uncle Scriptor explained they needed to know about pyramids, showed them into one of the smaller rooms off to the side. Callie's eyes roved across the

31

temple's shelves with all their stories and texts, and she licked dry lips in anticipation. Marcus smiled at her and decided she would be fine now, in here with all the books. And he had to concentrate on being as useful as possible. If there was even a hope that he could persuade the centurion to take them with him, it would at least partially hinge on how useful they were. Gallo had plenty of time for those who pulled their weight, but he would never have time-wasters in his unit, even if they were children.

As they stepped within, the priest hovered by the doorway, keeping a watch on the soldiers among the texts, but hard looks from both Gallo and Uncle Scriptor sent him away. The standard bearer strolled across and shut the door, and Gallo slumped into a chair and examined the huge map of the province that hung on the wall while Scriptor and Senex began to work through the racks of books and parchment scrolls.

'What shall *we* do?' asked Marcus in an excited voice, desperate to help as he looking around the racks and racks of scrolls. His sister grinned. 'I know this place quite well uncle. Potens uses this collection for work on aqueducts and roads. Tell me what you need.'

'You two take the bottom racks, then,' their uncle smiled. 'We want anything you can find on the pyramids.'

As Marcus and Callie set about the low scroll racks, Gallo sighed and grumbled at the map, complaining that he had no idea where to start.

'Most of the pyramids are in the north, of course,' Uncle Scriptor chattered as he perused the scrolls. Marcus made a mental note of that and put back the scroll he'd been perusing on the upper Nile region hundreds of miles to the south.

'And empty,' sighed the centurion, glaring at the map in irritation.

'And empty,' agreed Senex from across the room. 'In the south of the country there are a lot of tombs, but they are usually hidden and buried and those that can be found on top of the ground are only visible because they were dug out by robbers.'

'Pyramids, we want, not buried tombs,' muttered the centurion.

'Well,' Callie said in a light voice, unrolling a long parchment which spilled across the floor. 'Here is a scroll of all recorded pyramids, listed from north to south.'

'Good girl, Cal,' their uncle smiled, collecting the scroll and flattening it onto a table. 'That's a start.' Marcus redoubled his efforts to find something useful. His fingers rifled through ancient rolled parchments, as he peered at the small tags indicating what they were. With a grin, he double checked the last one and drew it from its space. 'And here's a record of the plundered pharaohs,' he said, flourishing another scroll and carrying it across to the same table. As Callie went back to the scroll racks in case of further finds, and Marcus wandered over to the centurion and his map, the two soldiers began work, Senex running down the list of plundered tombs while Scriptor marked the useless ones on his own list, placing a small coin from his purse next to each as they were named.

As the pair listed location after location, Centurion Gallo rose from his chair and tried to keep up with the ramblings by tapping the positions of those pyramids on the huge wall map, peering intently at the names as they ran down the river Nile. Marcus climbed onto a chair and quickly moved to point out the few positions the centurion missed.

After quarter of an hour, Senex finished his list and re-rolled the scroll, taking a deep breath.

'That leaves maybe two dozen possibles on my list,' said Uncle Scriptor brightly.

'But remember,' added Centurion Gallo, 'that just because they are not *known* to have been looted doesn't mean they *haven't* been. I have no list that says your purse is empty, but I bet it is now.'

Marcus sagged. 'So this has been no use, sir?'

'It's crossed off a lot of places, my boy,' Gallo replied encouragingly. 'You've done an excellent job, but we need to narrow it down a lot further yet.'

Callie peered at another scroll she had removed from a rack. 'I think I might have found what you're looking for, Uncle.'

The centurion sat up in interest. 'Go on, girl.' Marcus shifted his glance back and forth between the map and his sister fighting the irritation that she might be proving more useful than him, but simultaneously excited that she might have found something of help, which might improve both their chances of joining the adventure.

'It's called Hawara,' Callie said, unfurling the rest of the scroll on the table nearby as Senex and Scriptor arrived and began reading down it.

'Well it wasn't on the list, at least,' agreed the centurion. 'And what makes you sure it won't have been robbed?'

'Well two things, sir,' Senex noted as he perused the scroll Callie had located. 'The crocodiles and the maze.'

'Maze?' frowned Gallo.

'*Crocodiles*?' hissed Marcus.

'Yes,' beamed Callie, rifling through the texts. 'I remember Hawara. Herodotus the Greek and Strabo of Pontus both wrote about it.'

35

'Talk sense, girl,' grumbled the centurion irritably and Callie leaned back against the table. Marcus smiled and folded his arms. He knew that look in her eye. She was onto something and she knew it, and when Callie said she knew her histories and that something was important, it was always worth listening.

'Two Greek writers talked about the '*labyrinth*' at Hawara. Herodotus said it had *three thousand rooms*. A place like that might be tough for a thief to crack.'

'Or for a legionary,' muttered Gallo.

'And the pyramid stands on the rocks above the oasis and the city of Crocodilopolis,' added Senex.

'Croco-what-a-lot?'

'It's a holy city for the Egyptians,' Callie said. 'Sacred to their crocodile-headed god, Sobek. Crocs everywhere. They live in the rivers and oases and the priests even breed them there.'

'Wonderful,' grumbled Gallo. 'Alright, I concede it's unlikely it's ever been robbed. But then I wouldn't choose to rob the place myself, either.' He studied the map on the wall again in bafflement and huffed his irritation until Marcus leaned close and pointed at a city marked in a wide green basin southwards along the Nile.

'And it's about a hundred and fifty miles south,' muttered the centurion, nodding his thanks to Marcus. 'Long way.'

'Better than travelling to a nearer pyramid and finding it was actually looted a thousand years ago, sir,' pointed out Marcus, trying to pin something down and involve himself as much as possible.

'True. A hundred and fifty miles...' Gallo tapped his lip. 'About five days, then.' The centurion sighed. 'Well it's the best option. Hawara and Crocodile-oppollo-pops it is, then.'

The five investigators straightened and walked out of the room, Callie and Senex reeling off everything they had read and could remember of the pyramid and its labyrinth as Marcus and his uncle smiled at each other. They had a destination now, as well as a mission. Marcus only hoped that they had done enough already to prove their usefulness and that the centurion might consider taking them. The sun beat down mercilessly again outside and Gallo paused, blinking in the brilliance before they began down the steps towards the street.

'How much do you know about the local gods and their priests?' the centurion asked Senex. The old man officiated at all the festivals and rites of the unit's Roman gods, but Marcus wondered what he thought of Egypt's strange, animal-headed gods.

'About some of them, quite a bit. Not too much about crocodile cults, though, sir. Hawara might be dangerous.'

A voice at the side of the steps perked up.

'Hawara?'

The three soldiers stopped and Marcus and Callie stepped out to the side to see why. Close to the bottom of the slope sat an old man, possibly even older than the venerable Senex. He wore a rough white robe that had seen better days... *much* better, in fact. Marcus had seen well-tended oxen that were cleaner and neater than this figure. The man's hair, far from being the tight cut that was the current fashion in Egypt, was ragged, straggly and long, and his only other items of attire were dirty sandals, a shiny triangular pendant around his neck and the gnarled staff upon which he leaned like a crippled beggar.

'Rome does not approve of eavesdroppers,' snapped Gallo.

'But you talk of the city of crocodiles and the pyramid of the crocodile pharaoh?' the old man gave a grin with all three of his teeth on show.

Marcus glanced around for other listeners. Tomb robbing was not a business he thought it wise to broadcast around the city. But the only other people nearby were the native workers on the other side of the road, still unloading that string of carts and lugging the heavy crates into the warehouse. They were

38

paying no attention to the Romans and their unkempt companion.

'You speak Latin well, old man,' Senex pointed out suspiciously.

'I am a seer,' the dirty figure grinned and held out his arms as if to display himself. 'I tell many things. Of the future, of the will of the gods and even of whether a pretty girl will smile at you,' laughed the old man.

'And?'

'And a seer in Alexandria would have a very empty purse if he couldn't talk to the men of the legions.'

'I see.'

'You don't want to go to the land of the crocodile priests,' the old man said, his voice low and menacing.

Marcus stepped forward, frowning. 'Why not?'

'Dangerous, it is,' the old seer hissed. 'Crocodiles there have a taste for man and there are lots of them. And they're sacred there, too. Worth more to the people of the city than a man is, one of them sharp-teethed babies. Dangerous, is Crocodilopolis. They slither out of the water, through the fields, even walk the city streets. Save yourself a lot of trouble, centurion, and go somewhere else.'

'You seem to know the place well?' noted Callie interestedly.

'Ought to,' grinned the old man. 'From there, I am. *Born* there, I was.'

Senex leaned close to his centurion and cupped his hand to Gallo's ear, whispering quietly and receiving a nod in return.

'Then you shall come with us,' the centurion announced, pointing at the old man.

'Me?'

'You know the place well, and we need a guide. We will pay you the standard wages of a legionary scout for the duration. It will almost certainly be more money than you could make interpreting the will of Jupiter to the men of the fortress, certainly judging by your clothes.'

'But…'

'No buts, old man. You're coming. You can call it an order if you like. Or you could argue and we'll go and see the prefect of Egypt and ask *his* opinion…'

The seer's eyes widened as he began to shake his head. Turbo had a reputation for being a tough man – it was why the emperor had sent him to sort out rebellious, ruined Egypt. Marcus could almost see the old man weighing up his options and with a sigh the seer clearly decided that a city full of crocodiles held less danger for him than the prefect's office. Remembering that arched eyebrow at the dropped chainmail shirt, Marcus was fairly sure he was correct.

'Good. Senex, escort him back to the century and draw him the marching kit of a scout from supplies.' He turned to Scriptor as the elderly soldier escorted the old seer miserably back towards the city. 'We will go and see the prefect, lay out our plans and put in our requisition for everything we need.'

'Like pointy sticks?' the standard bearer asked quietly, and Marcus nodded, beset by a mental image of a hundred crocodiles snapping at his ankles. 'The lads are not going to be pleased about being sent off to rob a tomb, sir,' his uncle muttered. 'And when you throw crocodiles into the mix too, they're going to be less than happy.'

'A few days' march will set them straight. They'll be getting sick of garrison life anyway. We need to get them some exercise before they all go soft.'

'You could go by boat?' suggested Marcus.

'Too slow,' his uncle said, shaking his head. 'It'll be a five day march, but a boat upstream would take more like eight.'

'Who's going to look after us while you're away, uncle?' Marcus asked quietly, a slight hopeful edge in his voice. 'I mean, if the whole century are going…' He straightened, trying to look as fit and helpful as he could. Next to him, Callie broke into a disarming smile – the one Marcus knew she saved for when she really needed something.

Uncle Scriptor raised his eyebrows as he looked down at the two children at his heel. 'You could do with the fresh air and exercise, boy. How a lad can stay as pale as you in this sun is beyond me. And if you think I'm leaving this troublesome little girl in Alexandria to cause havoc while we're gone, you've another thing coming. No. Pack up your valuables, you two. You're coming to Crocodilopolis with the rest of us.'

Callie allowed her '*I want something*' smile to be replaced by the slightly smugger '*I got something*' one. Marcus tried not to grin like an idiot all the way back to the fort.

He failed.

CHAPTER 3

Callie's journal

Marcus' luck held and we joined Uncle's unit as it left the fortress. We have been moving south for two days through the Nile delta, heading towards the labyrinth and pyramid of Hawara, where we will break into the pyramid to find the gold prefect Turbo needs. The legion marched out very quickly and I did not have the time I wanted to find a book on the Egyptian language, if there is such a thing. I had hoped to study one on the journey and be proficient by the time we were at Hawara.

Instead, I will try to use my own skills whenever we see their writing and try and teach myself the basics. After all, I learned Greek in two months, and that uses a different script from Latin, so how hard can a language made of pictures be?

They say that where we are going is filled with crocodiles. The men of the legion seem to be terrified at the thought of it. I have never seen a crocodile up close. They don't really have them up in Alexandria – it's too cultivated and they can't live in the sea. But I've always liked the look of them. They seem to be lazy, like cats, and like to bathe in the sun. They might be dangerous in the wrong situation, as Marcus keeps muttering, but then so can a dog. I am looking forward to seeing them close up, so long as Marcus doesn't get all careful and try and stop me. Sometimes he is over-protective.

  We shall see.

Marcus maintained a dignified posture, his tunic and breeches dusty but his pride bright and shiny as he marched to one side of the head of the column, throwing in extra hurried steps to keep pace with the stomping feet of the legionaries. Next to him, Callie wandered along not even trying to manage a marching pace, often disappearing off to the side to smell a flower or chase one of the more curious ibis birds and then hurrying to catch up.

Their uncle Scriptor grunted as he hefted the bulky standard a little higher, his watchful gaze periodically rolling to the side to make sure Callie was still with them. The century of men had left the fortress of the 22nd legion yesterday morning and trudged south along the well-maintained road that ran beside one of the channels of the river Nile, stopping last night at the great 'City of Ships. The eighty-four men and their pair of helpers had been a little subdued, nervous over their destination. None of the legionaries were pleased at the prospect of robbing a tomb in a city full of crocodiles – well none of them barring Callie, who seemed happy enough at the idea. But by this morning the boredom and aches of the long march had taken over and the men had stopped complaining about their destination in favour of moaning about their feet and the endless dust clouds they kicked up. That and the weight of their heavy, hot armour under the burning Egyptian sun.

That same sun was beginning to sink towards the horizon in the west on this second day as the column arrived at their second stop-over – the town of Terenouthis. The settlement was small and largely unimpressive, huddled next to the river and dominated by a cemetery of huge tombs that was larger and statelier by far than the town it served.

As with everywhere on the journey, the centurion had selected places for their stopovers where the legions had previously built camps, so that there was no digging or building at the end of the day – just the setting up of tents and cooking of evening meals. It was bad enough marching to 'Crocodilopolis' to rob a tomb, without having to work hard every evening on the way there.

'What's the plan, sir?' Uncle Scriptor asked quietly, waving Callie back into the line from where she was investigating something in the reeds.

Centurion Gallo turned his head to the standard bearer, who was beginning to struggle a little in the heat with his heavy load and weighed down by the ceremonial leopard skin draped over his helmet. Scriptor was sweating so hard his face looked like a waterfall.

Marcus watched his uncle straighten under Gallo's gaze, and followed suit. If Scriptor could manage with the burden he carried, then Marcus wouldn't falter with virtually nothing to carry.

The centurion pointed at his second in command who was busy shouting at soldiers. 'Secundus can get the men settled in for the night. You, me and Senex... and the old fool,' he pointed at the tired Egyptian seer trudging along beside the soldiers, half way back along the column where he didn't have to talk to the officers and could grumble in peace, 'will be going into town briefly.'

'Into town sir?' Marcus cut in, in surprise. 'For supplies, sir? Will you need a porter?'

The centurion shook his head. 'Not for supplies, lad. Senex tells me there's a temple to this crocodile god in Terenouthis. I think it might be worth a visit, just to see what we're letting ourselves in for. Though I think it might be worth purchasing a cart if we can while we're here.' The commander glanced across at Callie, crouching by a colourful plant. 'Fancy a day off your feet tomorrow, you two?'

Marcus shook his head. 'I can manage, sir.' Behind him, Callie made a face as she plucked the bright flower. 'I'll ride in the cart with the old man.'

Uncle Scriptor nodded and smiled as he remembered deputy Secundus' face at the mention of crocodiles back in Alexandria. The deputy commander, apparently beset by a fear

47

of the scaly beasts, would be rather relieved to be staying in the camp and not attending a crocodile temple.

The low wall and ditch of the abandoned marching camp which would be their home for the night was a familiar sight as the legionaries approached. All over northern Egypt, whenever they had been out marching somewhere, the legions had built and spent the night in camps identical to this one and even Marcus had spent a few nights in them as the century had moved around for temporary postings.

As the centurion blew his whistle and Uncle Scriptor waved the standard, telling the men to stop marching the old seer hobbled over, muttering in his weird Egyptian language and rubbing his sore back. One of the bigger legionaries had taken pity on the old man and had carried his marching kit – all dangling from a long pole – for him, but still the old man had found it difficult to keep up with the soldiers' pace, and his feet were clearly aching badly. Marcus gave him a smug look. His own feet hurt like nothing he could have described, but he was not about to admit that in front of the soldiers.

'Tell us about Terenouthis,' Gallo said to the seer.

'What about it?' the old man grumbled.

'I understand there is a temple to the crocodile god there? I would like to visit it, and I would like you to join me.'

The old seer rubbed his eyes wearily. 'I won't ask why you actually want to get any closer to the place, but the priests might not see you anyway. Busy time of day, this.'

'They will see us,' the centurion said and then turned to his deputy, who was walking forward to catch them up. 'Secundus? Get the men settled in – tents up, meals on. We'll be back before it gets dark.'

As the deputy nodded and started giving out the orders, Gallo beckoned to Scriptor and Senex, and the two hurried over to join him, Marcus and Callie staying close to their uncle.

'We're going to go and find out about this crocodile god.'

Gesturing for the old seer to lead on, the centurion started walking across the dusty ground towards the town – little more than a collection of mud-brick huts, huddled round a few larger temples and a market. Uncle Scriptor shifted his grip on the heavy standard and leaned down a little.

'You two should stay in the camp.'

'But uncle, you might need us.'

The standard bearer gave Marcus a withering look, and he was just resigning himself to being sent back to help put up the tents when his uncle nodded. 'Alright. But remember: crocodiles are deadly. Stay alert and keep out of the way of any snappers. Be careful.'

Marcus nodded and gave a legionary salute that made his sister's eyes roll, relief flooding through him. He really didn't want to miss something as exciting as this.

As they walked, Gallo turned to the old seer.

'Tell me what you know about this god.'

The old man shrugged. 'Sobek is his name. He is one of the oldest and most powerful gods of Egypt. He protects the people and watches over the river, but he hates the people as much as he looks after them, and so the people both fear and love him back. He is proud and dangerous and often violent. Be very careful around his priests and worshippers… they have no love for Rome.'

Gallo sighed. 'I can't say that I have much love for crocodiles, but as long as they don't bother me, I won't bother them.'

'But you *will* bother them, centurion, for you go to rob the pyramid of the crocodile king.'

'Crocodile king?' asked Marcus, frowning.

The old man looked down at Marcus, his face darkening. 'The pharaoh Amenemhat the Third. He is the king in the Hawara pyramid. And he is the man who gave the whole oasis region to the crocodile god, not just the city at its centre. He had the temples built, and the breeding pools. He had the statues set up and invited the priests to rule the area. So you see: you have chosen a very dangerous pyramid to plunder, young one. Once again, I advise against it.'

'And once again, I will not change my mind,' snapped Gallo.

The old man shifted his dark look up to the centurion and waved his hands in a weird way. 'Then beware the wrath of the crocodile god. And for your own sake, don't tell the priests here what you're planning to do!'

As the six of them walked up between the first of the low houses and into the town, making for the temples that stood next to the river, old Senex cleared his throat with a sound like a dog scratching fleas. 'I'm looking forward to finding out more about this god. Always worth knowing about the local gods. Ours are *better*, of course. Jupiter will always rule the world, but the Egyptian gods are fascinating, with all their staffs, snakes, fake beards and animal heads.'

Marcus sniffed. Personally he couldn't understand how anyone could respect a god with a cat's head. He'd known a few cats in his time, and there didn't seem to be much room in their heads even for acknowledgement of the existence of people, let alone caring about them. Besides, if he admitted it, deep down in his soul he was starting to have doubts about the existence of even the sensible Roman gods. If they really cared about people, good men and women would not be lost at sea.

Uncle Scriptor still put offerings on the altar in the temple of Neptune, but clearly the god of the sea was not listening.

He took a deep breath, pulling himself out of such sad thoughts. He was with the legion now, even if he wasn't part of it yet, and he had a job to do. If visiting this Sobek temple could help the job, then that was what he must do.

'I expect there is a lot to learn from the priests here,' Uncle Scriptor said, 'if we know what to ask.' He looked down at Marcus and Callie. 'While we talk to the priests, you two do a bit of looking around. Stay quiet and be careful, out of the way of crocs, but keep your eyes and ears open. You might learn something useful.' He glanced across at the centurion's frown of concern and shrugged. 'The priests might not like Rome's army, but they might be a bit less guarded around children.'

'Then you two snoop a bit and listen carefully,' Gallo said to them, 'and we'll do all the talking with the priests.' The centurion, stretching, then turned to Scriptor and Senex. 'You ask the questions and try to foster a good relationship with them.'

Scriptor and Senex shared a smile and the small party passed the market – which was packing up for the day – and strode across to a temple that stood by the river bank. Of the three temples in the town, it was not difficult to see which one was theirs. The two great stone towers that stood either side of the gate each bore a carved and painted figure of a dark-skinned man with a green crocodile head. Marcus gave an involuntary shiver at the sight, though Callie simply gazed at it with curiosity. His sister made him chuckle sometimes. She was so tied up in the deep interest of things sometimes that simple factors like danger or fear never even bothered her.

Taking a deep breath, and suddenly more nervous than he had expected, Marcus stepped across the threshold and into the temple of Sobek. The wall in which the huge decorated gate stood enclosed a wide area on three sides, with the river itself forming the fourth. Behind that gate – and straight ahead of them – lay another smaller one, much the same, covered with pictures of the crocodile-headed god and thousands of the small 'hieroglyphics' – the picture writing of the Egyptians. This second gate marked the entrance to the main temple building, and the old seer paused, giving Marcus the opportunity to look around and take in his surroundings before they moved on.

As well as the main temple, there were other smaller buildings inside the enclosure, and a collection of shapes on the ground, marked out in low walls over in the more open area. A few men wandered around on their own business, each naked to the waist and wearing a short white skirt.

'Where now?' Gallo asked.

The old seer pointed at the main building. 'That is where the head priest will be. Don't ask me to go in. The crocodile god is frightening even to me.'

Gallo sighed and beckoned to the others as he spoke to the seer. 'Come with us to the entrance and introduce us to the priest, then you can go and hide in a corner if you want until we leave.'

The old man's shoulders slumped but he nodded and gestured for the others to follow him, walking towards the inner gate. As the men wandered off, the centurion leaned down to Marcus and Callie. 'Keep an eye on the seer as well, you two.' And then he was gone, hurrying after his men into the temple.

Marcus looked around the interior again. The dry, flat brown paving that made up most of the complex's grounds was dotted with strange tracks – two sets of parallel prints, with a central wavy line – and it didn't take him long to realise that they had been made by the feet and dragging tails of crocodiles roaming freely in the temple grounds! Were these people *mad*? He wondered how many priests were eaten each year by their own sacred crocodiles and shuddered, stepping away from the tracks only to find he was standing on more.

'Mad.'

'What's mad?' Callie asked brightly, moving next to him from where she had been examining the hieroglyphics on the temple walls, clearly missing Potens' wax tablet that she'd returned for the journey. Her vellum was too expensive to waste on notes, but a wax tablet could be scraped clear to start again.

'Having crocodiles wandering around in the courtyard. Maybe Secundus is right to be so scared of the things.'

Callie crouched and ran her fingers along the wavy tail track with a strange smile. 'I think they're cute.'

'That's because you're madder than a box of frogs,' grumbled Marcus, quickly looking around behind himself to make sure no toothy beast was sneaking up on them. 'Even a small one of those could really hurt you. If a big one got you cornered...'

But there were no man-eating reptiles hovering behind them. Probably the crocodiles all basked on the rocks and in the mud at the river's edge and, despite his nervousness, Marcus followed the outer wall, past the main temple building to where he could look over the river, preparing himself to run as though a thousand barbarians chased him if he got too close to one of the scaly, snapping nightmares. As he moved slowly and carefully so as not to startle anything dangerous, his sister bounced along happily at his side, trying to whistle a happy tune and mostly failing.

'Do you think their gods really are powerful?' he asked quietly.

'All gods are powerful, Marcus.'

'And yet you don't seem to be worried that we're going to loot a sacred tomb?'

Callie glared at him. 'Keep your voice down, brother. Remember where we are.' Seeing the guilty look on Marcus' face, she sighed. 'It's a matter of logic, Marcus. This crocodile god is an old god, worshipped by the Egyptians alone. Yes, annoying him might be foolish, but the very reason we are doing this is for the prefect, and through him, for Rome. That means we are doing the work of Jupiter, who is more powerful than Sobek by far, and whose people conquered theirs. Who would you rather defy? Sobek or Jupiter?'

Marcus pursed his lips. 'For preference neither.' His eyes picked out a particularly vivid painting of the crocodile god on the wall and he shivered again. As they passed the main temple, Marcus saw Scriptor, Senex and the centurion go inside with a priest, deep in conversation, and the old seer had wandered off on his own, leaving Marcus and Callie alone at this side of the courtyard.

Passing the rear corner of the temple, from which they could hear the chanting and singing of priests, Marcus gingerly approached the slope above the river, keeping as close to the complex perimeter as he could for safety. Callie looked up at the rows of images on that wall. 'I want to learn to read their pictures, Marcus. It's a pretty language, and it might help the mission, too. I like all the wavy lines.' She gestured to him and pointed at the wall. 'You see those three pictures... the *hook*, the *foot* and the *oil lamp*?' Marcus squinted until he found the line his sister was indicating, and then nodded. 'What do you think it says?' she asked.

He shrugged. 'Hook, foot, lamp?'

With a sigh, she rolled her eyes. 'I think that's Sobek, the name of the god. See how it's repeated and most often near the pictures of him. And if we know that means Sobek, then the hook is probably 'S' and the lamp 'K'. Shouldn't take long to learn this.'

Marcus rolled his eyes, shaking his head at his sister's perkiness in the face of such danger. Yes it was exciting, but a soldier had to recognise danger and not go all gooey about pictures of feet!

A few adult crocodiles, each twice as long as a man and as ugly as sin, lay motionless on the river bank, their horrifying razor teeth jutting both up and down outside their lips.

Occasionally, their eyelids would flicker and when one of them turned its head towards him, Marcus felt fear run up his spine in a shiver and realised he had taken a step back without meaning to.

'They're so sweet,' Callie gushed. 'Bet it's warm on those rocks. Did you notice that *crocodile* is a hieroglyphic picture too? I wonder how you say it.'

Marcus shot her a glare and then returned his gaze to the monsters by the river. Maybe it *was* foolish to attempt to rob a pyramid in a land sacred to these things and the god who shared their face? Briefly, he conjured up a picture in his head of the vulture-like prefect Turbo back in Alexandria and compared the Roman ruler of Egypt to the beasts on the mud in front of him. Even ignoring mighty Jupiter, and concentrating only on crocodile gods and prefect Turbo, it was a tough decision as to which was more dangerous, really.

He shook his head irritably. He was going to be a soldier. Soldiers had duties, and this century's duty was to bring the prefect a pharaoh's treasure, so that was what they would do. He had no doubt that Centurion Gallo would do his duty to the very end, no matter how many crocodiles he had to face, and how could Marcus ever hope to join the legion if he could not do the same? *"Come back with your shield, or on it."* Callie had told him that was what the Spartans used to say. Though he couldn't recall anything about "Come back with your shield or in the belly of a crocodile." Even the famous Spartan warriors might think twice about that one.

'You really think they're cute?'

'Just because something is dangerous doesn't mean it can't be cute.'

Marcus shivered again, suspecting that the reverse worked quite well sometimes, too. Callie could be as sweet as a honey-coated puppy, but that girl would walk him into a bear's den and would whistle happily while doing it. It was hard sticking to his promise to their parents some days. How did you go about protecting a girl who invited danger into her kitchen and poured it a cup of juice?

Taking a deep breath and gesturing for his grinning sister to follow him, he backed away slowly until he lost sight of the basking beasts and rounded the temple building. It had already become noticeably dimmer and the low, golden sun was no longer a circle, the bottom flattened by the western horizon.

He remembered hearing somewhere that the sun was pulled across the sky in a chariot, and wondered how the driver applied a brake at the other end. After all, if he didn't stop the sun, the sun would simply roll over the chariot and carry on going. He had half a mind to put the question to Callie, but stopped himself in time. Sometimes her explanations could be a little involved.

As they approached the front of the complex again, Marcus glanced with interest at the main temple building. Somewhere in there Gallo, Senex and their uncle were deep in conversation with the head priest, learning what they could about the crocodile god and his priests and temples. Intently, he peered into the entrance, which would be quite dim enough during the burning light of midday, but now, as the golden orb of the sun touched the western hills, was as dark as... well, as a crocodile's belly! He shuddered.

'Marcus!'

His head snapped round to see Callie pointing at a commotion over by the low brick walls, where priests in white skirts were huddled round in a group, shouting in their strange tongue. As he focused on the kerfuffle, Marcus was startled to realise that one of the voices crying out in the odd Egyptian language was the ancient seer they had brought with them from Alexandria.

What had the old man done? Callie was already pacing over to them, and Marcus, mindful of the danger into which she might be heading, turned his attention fully from the temple and hurried to catch up, just in case, jogging across the flat paving at his sister's heel towards the shouting. As they neared the area, Callie came to a halt and Marcus almost ran into her back, his eyes widening as he realised what the low brick walls were. The same now-familiar shudder ran up his spine again as he looked at the stumpy, walled circular areas.

Each of the three rings enclosed a pool of murky water with slabs sloping down into it. Each was home to a dozen baby crocodiles of different sizes. This was where they were breeding and nurturing the little monsters!

His heart pounding suddenly very fast, Marcus spotted the old seer by one of the pools, being pulled back by two of the priests while a small crocodile with jagged teeth clung onto his arm. As he and Callie watched, one of the priests produced some pink meat from a feeding bucket and waved it in front of the small beast, while the other grabbed hold of it around the middle.

As the baby croc let go of the seer's arm to snap at the pink meat, the priest yanked it back and carefully lowered it to the pool, its head turning this way and that, trying to bite the man who held it. As soon as it touched the ground, the lump of meat was dropped in front of it and, satisfied, the beast grabbed its morsel and swayed off towards the water.

The old seer was shouting something at the priests in his own language and Marcus was surprised to see that, while at first they were coming towards him angrily as if to tell him off for his interference, they stopped and simply turned and walked away.

The old man turned towards Marcus and Callie, his bitten arm tucked away inside his white robe. As he saw them, his face twisted into a frown and he stomped fast away from the breeding pool, hunched over with the damaged arm underneath his robe.

'I told you going anywhere near the crocodile cult was foolish,' the old seer snapped.

'*We* went to see the *adult* crocodiles and *we're* fine,' Callie grinned impishly, 'while *you* visited the *babies* and got bitten!'

The old man gave them a sour look. 'Still, I've decided I don't need your centurion's money. I just want to go back to Alexandria. If you had any sense, you would all go back to civilization and change your plans. The god Sobek is unforgiving and violent.'

'And you are a silly old man,' Callie replied, laughing. Marcus nodded and straightened in imitation of the centurion, screwing his face into a hard look. 'Rome needs your assistance for now, so paid or not, you're coming with us to Hawara. If you try to run away, Gallo will catch you. I'll tell him where you went.'

The old man gave Marcus an acidic look. 'Even Roman *children* are horrible,' he grumbled.

Callie took a step forward. 'Let me look at your arm.'

'My arm is fine.'

'Don't be silly. You were bitten by a crocodile. It may only have been a small one, but you might need a doctor and I've worked with the century's medic.'

'I told you I'm fine!' snapped the seer. 'I have had enough of this place. I will see you and your centurion friend outside.'

As the old man stamped off angrily towards the gate, Marcus took a deep breath and exhaled slowly. Surely the priests here must get bitten from time to time, so they must have someone who could help with wounds? Was the old man that afraid of Sobek and his crocodiles that he wouldn't even stay here long enough to have his arm seen to? But then, if he was, why would he visit the breeding pools in the first place? Still, Claudius, who was the medic for the unit, would probably be able to apply a salve to prevent infection when they reached the camp.

With a sigh, Marcus decided that the old man was probably only a short hop from being as mad as a bag of monkeys, watched him head for the huge gate, then turned and wandered back towards the temple. Callie peered after the old man with narrowed eyes until he disappeared from sight through the entrance and then hurried to catch up with her brother.

The bulk of the complex was now in shadow, the sinking sun's rays only catching the top of the building and the tips of the gate towers and obelisks with their hieroglyphics. The sun set fast in Egypt, and it was clearly time to go. It would be almost dark before they reached the camp as it was.

As they approached the temple building the three soldiers reappeared, accompanied by the priest and nodding their thanks as they departed. Marcus and Callie waited for them halfway to the gate and as they reached him, Marcus rubbed tired eyes.

'What did you find out, sir?'

'Oh, lots of things, my boy,' Senex smiled. 'Crocodilopolis is the home of the cult, you see. This pharaoh Amenemhat the Third was such a supporter of the cult that he changed his original plans to be buried with his family. He'd even already had a pyramid built near theirs, but then constructed another at Hawara, close to his precious Crocodilopolis. That's where the sacred croc itself is, and where the men in charge of the whole cult live. This pharaoh even named his daughter after the crocodile god!'

'So he was clearly mad,' Gallo added with a sigh.

'It seems that the locals are as frightened of Sobek as they are worshipful,' their uncle put in. 'They keep him happy, because the whole place is frightened of what will happen if he becomes angry.'

'I can understand that,' Mumbled Marcus, earning a superior look from his sister.

'Anyway,' the centurion announced. 'We are soldiers of Rome and we have our orders, so we go on, right into the mouth of the beast if necessary.'

'Did *you* hear anything useful?' Scriptor asked Marcus and Callie as the five of them headed for the gate.

'Not really,' Marcus replied. 'The old seer tried to persuade me that we should go back, but I told him we wouldn't. I told him you'd hunt him down if he ran.'

'Good lad,' Gallo murmured. 'We are not returning to Alexandria without a cart full of gold. If we go home empty handed, half an hour with prefect Turbo will make us wish we'd been eaten by a croc!'

The five of them passed under the huge gate and Gallo nodded to the figure waiting by the side of the path. The seer still clutched his arm inside his dirty white robe, which was now stained pink where his arm had bled a little into the material.

'What happened to him?' the centurion asked as they approached.

'Sobek bit him,' grinned Marcus.

65

Gallo turned a frown back and forth between the glowering seer and the grinning children and shrugged. 'Come on, it's getting dark and there are too many crocs around here for my liking.'

CHAPTER 4

The jaws snapped shut, razor-sharp pointy teeth interlocking horrifyingly. Callie scrambled away from the monster, wishing the centurion and his men were here... wishing anyone else was here. The crocodile's stubby legs stomped one pace forward and the jaws opened wide again, lunging to close on her leg as she scrabbled backwards in the dirt, trying hopelessly to get out of its reach. She stood no chance.

SNAP!

She felt the teeth brush her leg and almost weed herself in terror, felt her back thump up against the rock and realised there was nowhere else to go. Just her, with the rock behind and the monster in front. Time to...

Callie woke from her nightmare drenched in sweat and cold as stone, her heart pounding as though she had run a mile or two, her eyes wide in terror. Her mind had not quite yet accepted that she *had* woken and that the crocodile was nothing more than a bad dream, probably fuelled by Marcus' warning yesterday.

But crocs were so *cute...*

She was lying precisely where she had plonked herself down to sleep the night before, on her side and wrapped in a cheap blanket. Unmoving, her left shoulder stiff and achy from lying on it all night, she rolled her eyes. In front of her the leather of the tent obscured her view of the cemetery, and above the tent blocked out the stars. She could hear the grunting, rasping snore of Uncle Scriptor behind her, and the lighter sawing sound of Marcus' breathing beyond, which was comforting. On the rare occasions Marcus and Callie got to join the century on the march, they shared a tent with their uncle, as the centurion did with his deputy Secundus, while the rest of the unit's tents each held eight men, farting, sweating and snoring through the night.

Her heart started to thump faster again as she heard a pattering noise outside the tent over the general sounds of the camp at night. *What was that?* It sounded like the first drops of rain marking the start of torrential downpour. She'd experienced such weather on visits to Crete but not *here*. It *never* rained in Egypt. And the noises were too regular… like footsteps.

Her eyes were wide open now, her nightmare all but forgotten as she realised that someone or something must be creeping around outside their tent. How could that be, though, since this was a military camp and there were guards on watch everywhere to prevent someone getting inside the defences that enclosed them?

Something was wrong. She could feel it, the tiny hairs standing up on the back of her neck and making her shiver.

She tried to decide what to do next. She could simply stand up, grab her uncle's sword from the pile of kit close by and creep towards the door – she could lift the sword, even if she could never hope to swing the heavy blade. But what if whatever it was turned out not to be frightened away by the sight of a sword? What if it was six thieves creeping in with knives? Worse still, what if it was the monster from her nightmare?

The best option, she decided, was to turn over and nudge her uncle awake. Then the standard bearer would be able to face whatever it was, and Uncle would be well-rested already, judging by the snoring.

As quietly as she could, and very slowly so that she didn't alert whatever was creeping around outside, Callie turned over in her blankets, reaching out towards her uncle.

Her hand brushed a leathery snout and bounced off pointed, sharp, yellow fangs.

Callie screamed as her eyes focused on the crocodile right next to her, the soulless reptilian staring straight into her eyes.

It was not a traditional way to wake a Roman camp, but there was nothing she could do about that. When you turn over in the middle of the night after a horrible nightmare about crocodiles to find one staring at you, the only option is to scream.

Uncle Scriptor, trained professional soldier that he was, snorted in his sleep, not at all disturbed by his niece's scream, and rolled over on top of the crocodile, which Callie, despite her panic, was now beginning to realise was a small baby one like those they had seen in the temple yesterday. She felt the wee run down her leg anyway – her bladder had failed to make the distinction.

As her uncle snorted, grumbled something sleepily about being uncomfortable and rolled back away again, and Marcus leaped up, his wooden sword already in his hand, Callie stared in astonishment. The crocodile was now flat, its legs comically stuck out at the sides.

Callie remembered with a relieved smile that her uncle had a ridiculous habit of sleeping in his armour. Despite the discomfort, he said he felt better if he was always prepared for trouble, and Scriptor was *renowned* for his sleeping. The man could sleep on one leg, standing on the top of a column in a thunder storm. He had once slept through the first hour of a battle, and had only woken when someone came and shook him. That he could sleep in his armour was no surprise, though few others could.

71

The crocodile displayed clear dents and lines where the standard bearer's armour had squashed it.

Callie had trouble stifling her laugh as her brother stared wide-eyed at the small dead animal. Her uncle had defeated the monster and saved her from a nasty bite at the very least, and all without even waking up. It would be funny explaining it all to him in the morning.

What was less amusing, and a great deal harder to explain, was how the croc had got into the tent in the first place. They were a long way from the town and its temple, and even further from the river, which was where the crocs would normally be found. Out here snakes and scorpions were the more likely menace. A crocodile in this place was *really* odd.

She felt that shudder again as she remembered the temple earlier in the day and those giant images of the god, dark-skinned and imposing and with a crocodile's head. It irritated her to suddenly feel so unsure. Crocodiles had all been so cute until she'd had that nightmare and then found one inches from her nose! Sobek was apparently not a particularly nice god. But had they really insulted the god or his priests enough for this to happen?

Unless somehow Sobek already knew what the centurion was planning?

It occurred to her that although she had reassured Marcus that Roman Jupiter was bigger and more important than this Egyptian Sobek, Rome was a lot further away and Sobek was probably a lot closer. The realisation did not help return crocodiles to their previously cute state.

Shivering, she clambered from her blankets and to her feet. Gently, cautiously, she approached the small crocodile, which was perhaps as long as her arm, and prodded it with her toe. It failed to move. It was properly squashed, then.

Gingerly, slowly, Marcus crept across their uncle's sleeping form, bent and picked the animal up by the end of the snout, using only finger and thumb to pincer it shut as he lifted.

Callie's heart had started to slow but suddenly picked up its pounding rhythm again as she watched her brother with his wooden sword in one hand and a lifeless crocodile in the other. Outside, she could hear the shouts of the men as they reacted to her scream. They would be on their way to her tent. But she could also still hear that steady, regular pattering outside too.

Still holding the baby croc at arm's length, Marcus motioned her to stay still and be quiet, then sheathed his sword, crossed to the tent's entrance, fumbled with the tie with his free hand, and undid the flap, pushing the leather back and hurling the offending creature out onto the dusty ground of the camp. His heart almost thumped out of his chest as a shadowy shape darted across in front of him, and he stepped back in panic before he saw it again. The night outside was not truly dark. It never was out here in Egypt, as there was never enough cloud to hide the moon.

The silvery glow illuminated the creature that had spooked him and he smiled in relief as the stray dog that had clearly been making the pattering sounds picked up the squashed crocodile in its teeth and turned towards him. He could have sworn the hound was smiling at him in thanks for the treat.

'Don't mention it,' he breathed at the animal and watched, starting to calm down, as the dog lay in the dust about six feet from the tent's doorway, dropped the squashed croc between its outstretched paws and began to nuzzle curiously at it, trying to figure out how he could possibly eat this strange, hard morsel.

Marcus smiled. 'You'll have more luck if you turn it over.' He glanced back at Callie and motioned for her to come to the entrance. 'It's fine. Just a dog.' Callie edged next to him and the pair looked out at the mutt with the dead crocodile in its jaws.

'Are you alright?' came a deep, booming voice, and the children turned to see two of the unit's biggest, most muscular men coming to a halt in full armour and with weapons drawn.

'Yes thank you, Brutus and Maximus. A little croc managed to get into our tent, but Uncle dealt with it for us.'

The two huge legionaries frowned in confusion as they looked at the tent from which they could all still hear the standard bearer snoring with a sound like a German forester sawing logs.

'But you're safe?'

'Yes, Brutus,' Marcus confirmed, and Callie smiled. 'Thank you,' she added quietly.

The big legionary with the Spanish bull tattooed on both arms saluted smartly and turned to walk away. Maximus, an enormous Gaul with a flat nose and protruding forehead, made to follow, when he saw the scrawny hound, its ribs protruding from hunger, lying in the dirt, probing the crocodile.

'Scat!' he hissed and stamped a foot in the direction of the stray. The hound ignored him, turning the croc over in an attempt to find an edible, accessible part.

'Go on!' the big legionary hissed, stepping closer. 'Get out of here, mutt!'

Again, the dog ignored him, and as the legionary's enormous brow lowered in a frown, Centurion Gallo appeared in just his tunic with a drawn sword, took in the scene, smiled and waved the legionary away. 'Back to your post, Maximus.' A thought seemed to strike him as the man saluted. 'No, wait.

Go to the supplies and find some of the meat and the biscuits from the travel rations. Fetch a little of both for this poor animal.'

'Sir, he's a stray.'

'But he's hungry, and he'll not have much luck with that... *crocodile*?'

The centurion turned a concerned face to the children, and Callie pointed at the dead croc in the dog's mouth. 'It was in our tent. Uncle rolled onto it and squashed it before it could bite anyone.'

'Lucky,' Gallo said. 'What it was doing out here is a serious question. Still, it won't fill the dog, so we'd better do so, eh?'

Big Maximus narrowed his eyes, making Callie worry that the weight of his overhanging brow might cause him to fall over forward.

'With respect sir, my mum always said "never feed a stray else they follow you forever". Knew what she was talking about, my mum.'

'I'm sure your mother was very wise, Maximus. And probably patient. And undoubtedly large. But this poor animal is hungry, and he's no enemy of Rome, so I won't watch him starve in my camp.'

As Maximus saluted and walked off, a clear expression of disapproval on his face, Gallo crouched in front of the hound, who was trying to nibble at the croc's belly, but with little success.

'Don't worry, boy. Maximus is getting you some food.' He turned to the children. 'You two will make sure he's looked after, yes?'

'Oh yes,' Callie grinned, stepping forward and giving the stray a happy pat that sent a cloud of dust and dead fleas up into the air. Centurion Gallo smiled and the three of them watched the dog attempting to eat the croc, and nearly jumped out of their skin as a voice behind said 'Adopting strays, centurion?'

They turned, hearts thumping at the surprise, to see Uncle peering out of the tent.

'Sorry, Scriptor,' Gallo said. 'Did all the shouting wake you at *long last*?'

Uncle Scriptor frowned in confusion. 'Shouting? No, sir. No shouting. I think, though, I heard someone mention food. I'm peckish.'

Gallo laughed. 'Correct me if I'm wrong, Scriptor, but King Deiotarus – after whom our legion, the 22nd Deiotariana, is named – kept a famous pack of hunting dogs?'

'That he did, sir.'

'Then I think it only fitting our unit should have one. We'll take the sorry little devil with us and feed him up a bit. It'll be nice to have a mascot. Your nephew and niece have already agreed to look after him, and it'll be nice for Maximus to have someone he can talk to on his own level.'

Marcus and Callie laughed as their uncle broke into a yawn. 'What are you going to call him, sir?'

Gallo scratched his chin. 'I don't know.' He looked at Marcus and Callie. 'What do you think?'

Callie grinned. 'Dog.'

'A little basic, I'd say, but it fits I suppose.'

Scriptor chuckled. 'Saves a lot of trouble remembering names, eh, sir?' He shook his head with a sympathetic smile. 'I'm going back to bed, sir. Wake me up when breakfast arrives.'

As the camp dispersed once more to their beds or other tasks, Callie and Marcus crouched close to Dog in the moonlight. Callie had a calculating expression, and Marcus frowned at her.

'What are you thinking, sis?'

'That panicked me, and I've not been thinking straight. All this crocodile god stuff is making everyone too superstitious. I saw that thing in the tent and the only thing I could believe was that Sobek was angry. But I'm starting to think differently. I don't know why that thing was in our tent, but if a really powerful god was angry with us, I don't think he would send a baby crocodile.'

Marcus nodded. 'We'd have had a big killer, surely.'

'So why a baby croc.'

'At least it might have cured you of this happy little fascination with the creatures,' Marcus grinned. 'And you smell of wee.'

Callie kicked him hard in the shin and turned, stomping back into the tent to get some more sleep.

CHAPTER 5

Callie's journal

The closer we get to Hawara, the less certain I am of everything. Marcus is his usual wooden, enthusiastic self, failing to see more than one side to anything. But I am shaken. I had never believed myself a nervous girl, but that moment in the tent with the baby crocodile shook me badly, and I am having second thoughts about entering a place called Crocodilopolis, now.

I do not believe that the god Sobek is behind this, but whether it was gods or bad luck, walking into a city full of the things is not the exciting prospect it was a few days ago. I have hardened myself against things and resolved to let Marcus look after me as he feels he should. And once we are past the crocodiles and investigating the pyramid, I will feel better. We will find the gold, make Uncle and his unit heroes back at Alexandria, and please prefect Turbo.

But first, we must get past those crocodiles.

Marcus smiled appreciatively, looking around as he marched at quick-step-and-a-half alongside the head of the column. He had heard so many tales of the southern lands of Egypt over the years. Those who travelled here stayed close to the great river Nile, as the lands to the east and the west of that long waterway were mostly unforgiving desert. He had heard of the oasis surrounding Lake Moeris, of course – it was one of the most fertile areas of the province, where a lot of food was grown and a lot of papyrus made – but he had never hoped to actually see it.

The region was as green and verdant as the Nile's delta near Alexandria and bore very little resemblance to most of Egypt, which was brown, dusty and too hot to breathe comfortably. A small valley of green a few miles wide connected the huge oasis with the Nile valley, along which ran a canal dug so long ago that no one could remember who had done it.

He could hear Secundus shouting at the men at the back of the line, telling them to keep their knees up and not to fall out of step in the march and could even hear the occasional 'clonk' and yelp as the deputy batted them with his staff for getting it wrong.

At the front of the unit, he could also hear the low, muttered conversation between Scriptor, struggling in the heat under the weight of the leopard skin and the unit's standard, and Senex, struggling under the weight of his own brains. Marcus knew that they should be setting an example to the men and not chattering away like old women as they marched, and the look on the centurion's face suggested he shared the thought, but the two speakers had spent the last hour or two discussing Hawara and Crocodilopolis at length, and that was something Gallo was happy to allow. It was better that they were prepared, after all.

Dog pattered alongside them at the front of the column, keeping pace with the centurion, tongue lolling out and ribs still showing like the steps of a staircase despite the fact that Gallo and a few of the more sympathetic legionaries had been sparing him whatever they could each time the unit stopped to eat, and Marcus and Callie took every opportunity to try and fatten him up. Even after three days, passing through great and strange cities, Dog still seemed too thin to survive and was permanently hungry. But he was keeping up with them and looked happy and relaxed, and that was what mattered to him and Callie.

The same could not be said for the old seer who, though he had finally managed to get into the rhythm of the long trek, his feet plonking down in the dirt one after the other in a mechanical way, still looked utterly miserable. He rarely spoke unless someone asked him something, and spent the rest of the time grumbling about the journey and wanting to turn round and go back to Alexandria. Despite the presence of the cart they had purchased at Terenouthis, and in which Callie spent much of the journey to save her legs, the seer stumped along sorely. Despite initially allowing the old man to ride along in the cart, far enough back for his constant complaining to be out of the officers' earshot, twice now the old fool had fallen off the cart and, harbouring the suspicion that both falls had been attempts to run away, Gallo now required the seer to march up front with the rest, where they could keep an eye on him.

'Is that it?' asked Senex suddenly, pointing off to the right.

Marcus looked where the veteran soldier was pointing. On a high, rocky area that overlooked the green valley, lumps of broken stone and parts of ancient, shattered walls almost obscured the bulk of a huge white triangle that rose into the blue sky only a quarter of a mile away.

'You have good eyes,' grunted the old seer, 'though your brain is still addled if you want to stay here and not go home to the comfort and the sea breeze in the north.'

Marcus ignored the old native's complaints and Senex's snapped reply, and narrowed his eyes at the pyramid and then down to the deep, sluggish waterway that lay in between. They were very close. 'Where do we cross the canal to get to it?' he asked.

'There are bridges,' grumbled the old man.

Gallo shook his head. 'We'll go to the pyramid later. In fact we will camp near it tonight. First, though, I want to go into the city and speak to the officials there. We might be here for a day or two and there could be trouble if they don't know who we are and why we are here.'

'There might be more trouble if they *do* know,' pointed out the seer, folding his arms.

'Take us to the head man in the city,' the centurion said, pointing ahead among the trees and fields. 'How far from here is Crocodilopolis? You said it was near.'

'Maybe three or four miles,' the old man shrugged. 'The man you need to speak to is the head priest of Sobek, in the great temple.'

'I thought you were going to speak to the local official, in charge?' Marcus asked the centurion.

'The high priest of Sobek *is* the man in charge,' explained the seer.

Gallo frowned. 'But there's a Roman cavalry unit based somewhere nearby. And this is the capital of a district. It should have its own civil leader.'

'It does,' explained the old man quietly. 'But he is also the high priest of Sobek. No one in the whole oasis has more power than the temple. They were here thousands of years before you Romans, and they know the crocodiles will still be here long after you have gone.'

Gallo sighed. 'Alright, then. Leads us to this priest.'

The century marched on into the rich, green landscape of the oasis, fig and date trees clustered around good fields. The men began to eye the fruit hungrily, licking their lips in anticipation of something more pleasant to eat than the rations of hard biscuit and salted meat they carried with them. As the road rounded a corner, Marcus' step faltered and he almost stopped in his tracks as his eyes fell upon the huge statues of crocodile-headed men that stood on either side of the road, watching the approach for people visiting the holy city of crocodiles.

His heart thundered in his chest as he spotted one of the *real* beasts swaying around in the greenery behind the statue, its tail swiping this way and that. He hadn't given much thought to the actual animals recently, despite what had happened in the tent back at Terenouthis, but now he remembered the others telling him that crocodiles walked the streets here. It sounded like that temple with the baby crocs, but worse. He was secretly pleased to see Callie shrink back at the sight too. Her encounter with the baby crocodile in their tent seemed to have killed off her interest in the beasts fairly convincingly.

Dog was suddenly walking so close to him that he could feel the hair of his scruffy coat on his shin. Clearly Dog had no more love of the creatures than the Romans.

As they approached the statues, Gallo gestured to Scriptor, who dipped his standard to the left and the whole century of men edged to the far side of the road as they marched, moving around the long, dangerous creature in a wide arc, and away from the canal, which had turned north after the pyramid.

Passing by, all thought of delicious fruit gone from the minds of the men as they stared at those jaws which could bite through a man in one go, Marcus peered over the top, beyond the road and the croc, to where he could just see the wide irrigation channel which cut its way through the green, supplying water to the fields. Sure enough, dozens of bumpy, long shapes lay on the banks of that waterway, their tails occasionally flicking as they basked in the sun.

Callie suddenly shuffled very close to him.

'Marcus?'

He turned to face her. 'Yes, sis?'

'I don't like this place. I don't like it, and it's starting to make me shiver.'

Marcus sighed. It never ceased to surprise him how Callie, who lived for the fact and understanding in her books, could still manage to be so flighty and superstitious at times. He pointed back to the column. 'Don't be nervous,' he whispered so that the others couldn't hear. 'We're surrounded by soldiers. Gallo won't stop until the mission is complete, and if he can do it so can we.'

Callie's face hardened. 'Marcus, you're not a legionary. You might think you are, but you're still a boy, and this is getting scary.'

He fixed his sister with a steady gaze. 'I thought you had changed your mind about Sobek, and decided that he wasn't behind that little attack?'

Callie glared at him. 'There doesn't have to be a god involved for it to be scary, Marcus. A dozen crocodiles are scary enough.'

In truth Marcus' flesh was crawling as though it wanted to get off, and the ever-increasing number of man-eating beasts was threatening to make him cry a little, but his future was to serve with these men, and he *would* not show fear!

'Stop talking like that,' he said, trying to sound reassuring and sturdy rather than worried and whingey. 'There are eighty trained soldiers with us. We're safer here than anywhere else.'

Callie, clearly unhappy, opened her mouth to argue, but Marcus turned away from her and concentrated on not sweating at the sight of yet more crocodiles. The episode in the tent had clearly scared her a lot more than he'd realised – not just out of her fascination with the things, but actually into an ongoing proper fear. He would have to watch over her carefully in this place.

Another mile passed without a word, every man in the column keeping all his attention on the road ahead and the land to either side, aware of the slightest movement. It quickly became clear that the crocs were everywhere, some just lying in the fields or by the side of the road. When Gallo spotted a particularly big and dangerous looking specimen lying right in the middle of the path, he had the standard waved again and the entire century of men tramped off across the thick dirt of a field in order to pass the beast without getting anywhere near it. Dog issued a low growl all the time, keeping his eyes on the thing, staying so close to Marcus he kept falling over him.

Another mile of watching the terrifying animals and keeping out of the way of the ones nearest the road, and Marcus finally spotted Crocodilopolis itself, rising up between the trees and above the fields. While the low-quality houses of the peasants were the usual squat, brown buildings made of mud bricks, there were a number of larger structures of stone among them, and it came as no surprise to see the pair of crocodile-headed statues standing on either side of the road just outside the city, guarding it from intruders.

The pointy tips of obelisks rose above most buildings, and many towering *pylons* – the towers which stood on each side of a temple gate – could be seen, meaning there were at least six temples here.

His nerves starting to twitch, Marcus stayed close to his nervous sister and kept in step as Gallo led the century towards the town along the dusty road, waving at the miserable looking seer to join him.

'What?' the old man snapped childishly.

'When we get there, I will take Senex and Scriptor in with me to talk to the priest.'

'So?'

'I want you to come with us, too.'

'Me?' The old man shook his head. 'No, no, no, no. Not me. I'm not going in there.'

'Yes you are,' said Gallo, quietly but forcefully. 'The *children* are coming with us, and they're not scared.' Marcus did his best to look tall and brave, though in truth, he was quivering at the thought, and Callie certainly *looked* scared. Still, he reasoned, in this place, even standing on the road could get you eaten by a crocodile, so there was no reason the temple would be more dangerous than anywhere else.

'Anyway,' the centurion went on, speaking to the seer. 'None of us speak your language, and this head priest might not speak Latin. We might need you. Anyway, I'm paying you well for this.'

'I told you to keep your money and send me home.'

'You are coming in with us,' the centurion said flatly. 'No arguing. But be on your best behaviour. I don't want to make the priest angry. We want peace with the locals.'

'Then don't go robbing their tombs,' grumbled the old man.

Gallo ignored the seer as the man continued to moan about everything he could think of, and led the unit into the city. Marcus looked around with interest, taking in everything he could of his surroundings, while keeping Callie close at his side, her eyes wide. The ordinary folk of Crocodilopolis went about their own business and here and there they could see the sharp, pleated white skirt and white hat of a priest. Some of them, presumably the more important ones, were wearing leopard skins much like the one Scriptor had draped over his helmet, though they wore them wrapped around themselves like a thick, furry cloak, with the paws tied together at the front to keep them on. Some had a long, colourful staff which they rapped on the ground as they walked. Some even had a strange little fake beard on their chin which had to be kept in place with a string hooked behind their ears, which made Marcus smile despite his nerves.

His eyes went wide with surprise as he saw one of the larger crocodiles, maybe twice a grown man's height in length, emerge from a side street. *Right in the middle of the town*! The locals – even the poorest peasants – just sidestepped a little to stay out of the reach of its jaws, should it decide it had walked far enough and now fancied a snack. Gallo and his trained and dangerous soldiers had walked half a mile to get round one of these things, yet a man who made pottery just turned his little hand-cart full of bowls so that he was a little further away from its lazy jaws.

Marcus found himself wondering whether this was because they were so used to crocodiles here that they were no longer scared of them, or was it perhaps that because they worshipped the great croc god here, he kept them from being eaten?

Either way it made no difference to the Romans who did not enjoy the favour of Sobek, and who were not used to having a fourteen foot man-eater crawl past while they were sitting on their doorstep and eating their lunch. Dog was once again so close as he walked that Marcus could feel the hair of the coat scratching his leg and swore he felt a flea bite his shin.

The century's nerves continued to tense as they passed through the town and finally arrived before the high towers and imposing gate of the great temple of Sobek at the town's centre. The temple was surrounded by a pond with gently-sloping stone banks, a little like a shallow moat. It was no shock to any of them to see dozens of crocs lounging around in the water or on the edge, sunning themselves and watching the approaching Romans, probably trying to decide which one looked tastiest. Marcus did his best to look fatty, stringy and unappetising, hoping that the lean, muscular figure of Gallo nearby, wearing centurion's bright red too, looked a lot tastier to the beasts. Callie was suddenly almost as close as Dog, sandwiching herself between Marcus and their uncle for safety.

Holding their breath, Marcus and Callie accompanied the officers at the head of the century across the causeway that led to the gate and passed inside the high wall of the temple complex.

Much like the one at Terenouthis, this place had a large temple building inside with its own high pylon gate, and a few smaller buildings around the edge. Of course, it was on a much larger scale. The main temple alone was more than twice the size of the Terenouthis one, and the buildings around the wall were each larger and more impressive than at the other city. The main difference, of course, was that there was no river

Nile here, and the wall completely enclosed the complex, with the croc-filled moat outside that.

The other difference was that as well as the low-walled breeding pools which Marcus could see at the rear, there was a larger version – huge in fact – with a small, decorated temple at the edge. As Marcus watched, he almost jumped out of his skin when he spotted the pool's occupant. A single crocodile, larger than any he had ever seen, suddenly reared out at the edge of that pool and looked straight at him. Again, he felt the distinct urge to wee himself, but tensed as he watched the beast. At maybe twenty feet long, it was *enormous*. More than that, though, it seemed to have been adorned with golden bands round its legs and a huge gold thing around its middle that looked a little like an armoured breastplate. And attached to all this gold were enough precious jewels for prefect Turbo to rebuild half of Alexandria. The look on Gallo's face said it all: he had no intention of getting within snapping distance of that thing, no matter how much gold it wore. Marcus found himself wondering how the priests managed to get these gold fittings on the beast in the first place. Either they were insanely brave, or they had let him eat one of them while the others worked.

'Prefect Turbo would like all that gold, sir.' He shuddered, and Callie huddled even closer, her breathing rapid.

The centurion gave Marcus a hard look. 'If prefect Turbo wants those, he'll have to come and get them himself!'

Marcus nodded emphatically.

'Ignore Petsuchos,' the old seer said unhappily. 'You need to go into the main temple.'

'Petsuchos?' Marcus replied, unable to take his eyes off the animal.

'The lord of crocodiles, sacred to Sobek. He is immortal and holy.'

'And terrifying,' Marcus added, turning to look for Secundus, only to see that the deputy had pushed his way into the middle of the men, just in case Petsuchos suddenly fancied a Roman meal. Now he would have to get through a few legionaries before he could eat the deputy.

'Come on,' Gallo pointed at the main temple. 'Senex, Scriptor and the seer with me. Secundus, you take the men and wait over near the gate, and keep Dog with you. We don't know whether a stray dog will be welcome in a temple.'

Leaving the deputy to organise things out there, Gallo took his two other officers and the old native with him, and strode to the central temple's entrance. Once again, Marcus and Callie hurried on behind them, and the centurion paused, noting the presence of the children. 'I don't think this will be a safe place for them, Scriptor.'

The standard bearer caught the desperate hope in Marcus' eyes and turned back to his commander as Callie latched tightly onto his leg.

'Neither is the outside, sir. Might we take them in?'

Gallo bit his lip for a moment and then nodded his agreement, much to the Marcus and Callie's relief. The four men and their two young accomplices marched on to the entrance. Two locals with smooth white hats and leopard skin cloaks frowned as they approached, and whispered to each other, pointing.

'We are here on the authority of prefect Turbo, governor of Egypt,' the centurion announced, saluting them. 'We need to see the high priest.'

The two Egyptians muttered something to each other, and then one of them turned to the six newcomers and rattled out a few sentences in his own language.

Gallo shook his head, unable to understand a word, and turned to Scriptor and Senex, standing at his shoulders. The old seer was behind them and off to one side, where Marcus kept a vigilant eye on him. He'd been told to watch the seer once before and almost missed him being bitten by a croc. He wouldn't make that mistake again.

'What did they say?' Gallo asked the old man.

The native stepped forward.

'They said that the high priest, Inkaef, is not here. He is away from the city on some business of the cult's.'

Gallo took a deep breath. 'Then tell them we need to speak to his second in command.'

The seer chattered away in Egyptian at the two priests, who quickly replied and then pointed inside.

'What was that?' the centurion asked.

'They said the priest in charge of mummifying crocodiles will speak to you. In the high priest's absence, he is in charge.'

'*Mummifying crocodiles*?' Marcus asked in surprise.

'Oh yes,' the seer replied. 'The crocodile is as sacred here as the pharaohs were. When they die they are turned into mummies and buried in tombs of their own.'

'You people are absolutely mad, you know that?' the centurion shook his head as they were led inside by the two priests. Through rooms, doorways and chambers they were taken, through courtyards surrounded with columns and into the smaller rooms at the rear. Every wall and every column was carved with pictures of the crocodile god and of priests and pharaohs and vultures and covered in the *hieroglyphic* language of the Egyptians. And they were all painted in bright, vivid colours. Her nerves apparently temporarily forgotten in the presence of her latest fascination, Callie studied the writings as they passed with interest, pointing out to her brother the familiar *hook, foot, lamp* of Sobek's name in various places.

Finally they paused at the entrance to a room, where the two priests entered and rattled away in their weird language with someone inside. Gallo looked expectantly at the seer, but he apparently wasn't listening, instead hopping from foot to foot and looking around nervously as though desperate to leave.

The two priests reappeared and gestured for them to enter. They did so – Gallo expectantly, Scriptor, Senex and Marcus alert and watchful, Callie, in the absence of crocodiles but the presence of hieroglyphics, taking everything in with interest, and the old seer reluctantly, clearly wishing he was anywhere but here.

'Greetings, holy man,' Gallo said respectfully. The mummifying priest was even older than the dribbling ancient seer they had brought with them, though he was done out in all the best priestly kit, even down to gold armbands and a thick gold collar studded with black and blue stones.

The priest chattered away and the seer started to translate without being asked.

'He asks what business Rome has here.'

The centurion took a deep breath. 'Alright,' he said to the seer, 'tell him this, but do it as nicely as you can:'

98

He turned an ingratiating smile on the senior priest. 'We are not here to cause trouble or harm to the priests of Sobek, nor to your temple, town, or crocodile-mummy tombs.'

The old priest nodded, suspiciously.

'Nor do we wish to cause any harm to the people of the oasis.'

Another suspicious nod.

'But there is a pyramid lying between here and the Nile, at the hill called *Hawara*, and the governor requires the treasure buried within it for the good of Egypt, to rebuild the damaged city of Alexandria. We must have pharaoh…' he paused.

'Amenemhat the Third,' supplied Scriptor helpfully.

'Amenemhat the Third's treasure for the prefect.'

The priest waited as the dusty seer translated, watching the old man intently. When the last words echoed around the room, the priest started shaking his head, and then began to rant in Egyptian.

'He says no,' the seer translated. 'Absolutely not. The pyramid is that of the crocodile king and is sacred. You must not touch it.'

Gallo sighed. 'I have no choice, and neither do you. We all have to do what the prefect tells us to. He has told *me* to get this treasure, and I will do it. I have a century of Roman legionaries with me, and a cavalry unit is based nearby, so do not try to stop us, I warn you.'

His face softened. 'Tell him that I am truly sorry that I have to do this, and it is not our habit to rob tombs. But Alexandria is a burned out ruin and must be rebuilt for the good of Egypt. And the money for that has to come from somewhere. Ask him if he is willing to supply guides or workers or helpers who know the area?'

The old seer did not look at all pleased at the words he had been given to translate, but he did it anyway, sullenly. The priest was shouting his reply before the translation had even ended and the seer had to hurry to keep up.

'He says absolutely not. The king Amenemhat was patron of Sobek's cult. He is the most sacred of all the pharaohs and you will not take the treasure.'

'Yes I will.'

'He says that if you try, you will bring down a curse upon you and the crocodile god will consume you.'

'I'm more worried about *real* crocodiles consuming me,' grumbled the centurion, who simply straightened with a sigh and saluted. 'Then we are done here. Thank the priest for his time, but warn him not to interfere with Rome's business.'

A low, menacing growl attracted Marcus' attention and he looked down in surprise. He thought Dog had stayed outside with Secundus and the men, but the stray was standing by his side, snarling at the old priest. Somehow that made him feel a lot better about the whole thing. He reached out and patted Dog's back and the animal moved close to his side. Callie was busy staring at the images that covered every flat surface of the wall in interest.

As the centurion turned and began to stride away from the room, out of the temple, and the two children followed on, Callie nudged Marcus.

'What?'

'I think I'm getting the hang of their language. There are some sounds that escape me, but I think I've Identified the name of the pharaoh here and there under pictures that have to be of him, so that gives me new letters to work with.'

'Fascinating,' muttered Marcus uninterestedly.

'There was one other thing,' she said, as they emerged into the daylight.

'What's that?'

'Did you see the mummification priest fiddling with his pendant?'

'No.'

'It was a triangular pendant on a chain round his neck, almost hidden by that gold collar. He was playing with it nervously, as though he was trying to hide something, or was lying to us.'

'Maybe you should tell the centurion.'

Callie nodded and reached out to tug on Gallo's arm as he left the building.

'What is it, girl?'

'I know this sounds odd, sir,' she said quietly, 'but I'm pretty sure there was something the priest in there wasn't telling you.'

Gallo nodded irritably. 'I would not be at all surprised. Come on. We're getting no help from here. Let's leave this crocodile nightmare and get to the pyramid. Time to see what we're up against.'

Marcus felt the thrill of excitement, heavily tinged with fear, run through him.

The pyramid at last...

CHAPTER 6

Callie's journal

We are here. Marcus seems to think that this is it and that by morning we will be laden with gold and treasure and making our way back north. It is an attitude shared by a lot of the men, I think. Only Uncle, Potens and Senex seem to see it the same way as me: we have arrived, but now the real work begins. Until now all we have had to do is get to the pyramid, which even Dog could do.

Now, though, we have to get into the pyramid. These are ancient tombs. I read about them a lot back home, and I know that once the pharaoh was buried in them, they were sealed tight to prevent tomb robbing. Worse still, they are rumoured to be filled with traps to catch unwary thieves. And before we meet those traps, before we even have to break our way in, we will have to work out where the entrance is. I have made a little progress with my notes on the native language, and I think I can begin to pick things out on the painted walls when we get to them, but even that requires us to get inside first.

This might not be as simple as it seems.

'So this is a 'labyrinth', is it?' Gallo said, apparently unimpressed.

Marcus and Callie looked around at the ruins on the bluff overlooking the canal which they had seen when they first arrived at the oasis. All that seemed to remain were small lumps of stone and low, broken stretches of wall. Certainly nothing maze-like. Even kneeling down, a man would be able to see right the way across the place. Most of the century of men were on the stony ground nearby, gathered into groups of eight to eat their hard biscuit and salted beef, and only a few guards and the officers strolled about. The children stood among the shattered structures with the centurion, as well as Senex and their uncle.

The sky was already starting to lose the sun's brilliance as the afternoon wore on, and the unit would soon have to think about their camp site for the night, but there were a few hours of light left yet and Gallo wanted to find out as much as possible before the sun set.

Marcus shrugged. 'It feels strange, though, sir. Makes me tingle.'

Scriptor nodded. 'Me too. And just because there's no maze here now doesn't mean there wasn't a labyrinth once. Don't forget that those writers Callie mentioned who spoke about the labyrinth were around hundreds of years ago. Maybe there was an earthquake?'

Marcus nodded, his eyes straying around the site. Beyond the ruins a slope descended to the canal below. If he squinted, he could make out Crocodilopolis in the distance among the green. And then, at the other side, there was the pointed bulk of the pyramid. Perhaps a hundred and fifty feet tall, it was an impressive monument, with its smooth, sloping stone sides.

'Potens!' the centurion shouted, cupping his hands around his mouth, and then waited until the man came jogging out of the gathered eating parties. Potens was the unit's trained engineer, capable of overseeing most jobs as they were required. He had planned aqueducts, built bridges, dug channels and even built barrack blocks with the aid of the other men. A small man, Potens was broad across the shoulder, giving him a look that suggested he might be top-heavy enough to fall over in a strong wind. He was also Callie's best friend in the unit and as the heavy-set man ambled up, Marcus' sister scurried across to stand next to him.

'Sir?' the engineer saluted as he came to a halt in front of his centurion, patting Callie fondly on the head.

'I need your opinions, Potens. Firstly, and less importantly, here. This is supposed to be a labyrinth. What do you make of it?'

Potens turned in a slow circle, scratching his head, and then crouched down to examine a ruined wall and rubbed at the dusty stone.

'This was no maze, sir. It was a big place with quite a few rooms, though. Well decorated and painted, too. The sort of place... sort of like the inside of the temples, sir.'

'So there's no labyrinth here?' Marcus asked.

Potens grinned and tapped the side of his nose like a man with a secret. 'I didn't say that. I said *this* was no maze.'

Gallo harrumphed irritably. 'Make yourself clear, soldier.'

'Well sir,' Potens smiled, producing his wax tablet and illustrating his words as he talked, 'this was a large, palatial sort of temple-type place. But I'd be willing to bet there's something underneath. This floor is made of tightly placed stones. Really heavy ones. It'd take a big wooden frame to lift them, but that suggests to me that there's another level underneath. Otherwise they could just have built it using the rock of the ground here.'

Callie smacked her forehead with the palm of her hand. 'That's right!' She shook her head. 'Of course! Herodotus said that there were three thousand rooms, but that half of them were underground.'

'There were certainly not three thousand rooms on top,' Potens said, looking around. 'Maybe a hundred or so.'

'Well, writers always exaggerate,' smiled Callie, nodding at the writing tablet in the engineer's hands. 'But even if he did, that might mean there are another hundred rooms underneath.'

Potens nodded. 'Maybe. This top level was demolished about three or four hundred years ago, judging by the decay. I would think that a lot of the stone ended up building the more impressive bits of Crocodilopolis.'

'Right,' announced the centurion. 'The labyrinth is interesting, but it's the pyramid we want to get into, so let's go have a look at it. Potens, come with us.'

For the next half hour, the small group walked slowly around the pyramid until they returned to the start, then turned around and did it again in reverse, and then a third and a fourth time, all the while looking closely at the sloping stone sides. As the grown-ups walked, Marcus and Callie examined the building with them, while Dog ran in small circles having fun in the sand.

Every face of the pyramid was smooth and flat, with no marks or holes.

'So how do we get in?' Gallo sighed.

'Well at least there being no entrance is good news, sir,' Callie announced.

'Really?'

'Well yes, Centurion. If there's no hole into it, it seems very unlikely that it has ever been plundered before. It looks like we were right and the tomb's treasure will still be there with the old pharaoh.'

'Come on,' said Gallo and strolled back across to where they had first been standing on the labyrinth ruins. Nearby, close to the slope, the seer sat huddled with his arms around his knees, looking down to the canal.

'Old man!' Gallo bellowed at him. 'Come here a moment.'

The seer turned and, seeing the centurion beckoning, slowly rose to his feet, rubbing his knees. As he wandered over, Gallo scratched his forehead.

'We're having difficulties. What have you been doing?'

'Watching all the crocodiles down by the water,' the old native grumbled. 'There are nearly as many of them as there are of you.'

Gallo shivered and turned. He spotted Secundus chewing on a lump of beef while he looked in the direction of the canal with alert eyes and waved to him.

'Get the men round the other side of the pyramid and start making camp over in the sandy bit. Just leave a few heavy lads here in case we need a hand.'

'Why, sir?' Secundus frowned. 'Where you are now, we've got a good view and hard ground.'

'And a lot of restless crocodiles. Let's not camp close enough to annoy them, eh? Get the men away and set up camp beyond the pyramid.'

As Secundus saluted and went off to rouse the troops, the centurion turned back to the rest.

'You should give up and go home,' the old native grumbled. 'I'm getting sick of telling you.'

'We are not leaving without a cart full of gold for Turbo,' announced Gallo flatly yet again.

'Then I don't know what you're going to do,' the seer grumbled.

'Potens, what do you know about pyramids? You've had a look at them in the north whenever we've been near them.'

The engineer pursed his lips. 'Weeeell,' he drawled. 'The entrance is low down in all pyramids I've seen. And it's almost always on the north side, though I've heard of a few different cases.'

'So if we just look at the north,' Gallo mused, 'we narrow it down to just more than two hundred feet. And if we have to start moving the outer stones to find the entrance?'

Potens gave him a dark look. 'Well, sir... the first thing we would have to do is work out where the ground is.'

'But we're standing on it,' puzzled Marcus.

'We are standing on the *current* ground, but dust and dirt and sand continually settle in the wind, and the ground rises all the time.' The engineer smiled. 'I have often wondered where it all comes from in the first place. Anyway, the question is: where was the ground at the time the pyramid was built. Because that will be where the entrance is.'

'You're so clever,' grinned Callie next to him, and Potens smiled down at her.

Gallo's shoulders slumped. 'So it could be more than two hundred feet long?'

'It could be a *lot* more,' the engineer confirmed.

'Alright. And what then?'

'Then we would have to remove blocks of the facing stones all the way along. Each one will weigh more than a cart and oxen, so we'll have to build a big wooden frame with some ropes to move them. I'm afraid, centurion, that it is not going to be a quick job.'

'Scriptor shook his head. 'There must be an easier way. I think this labyrinth is the key. Why build such a big, complicated monument if it was not connected in some way? I think the answer is under our feet.'

'Maybe,' Gallo nodded, 'but that in itself is almost as big a job as the pyramid. I think that without more information, we are at a dead end.'

Potens and Scriptor looked at him, nodding unhappily.

'Then go back to Alexandria,' the old seer urged them. 'Go and read your books again and find an easier pyramid somewhere where there are fewer crocodiles.'

Gallo rounded on him, pointing an angry finger. 'I told you: we are not going back without a cart load of gold.'

'Then what do we do, sir?' Marcus asked quietly. There didn't seem a way out of this.

'We ask the gods for help,' old Senex replied. If men cannot do it, then perhaps the gods can. We need to hold a sacrifice and see if they will help us get inside.'

'Maybe we could sacrifice a crocodile,' Gallo grumbled, glancing across towards the slope and the canal, which they now knew to be full of the monsters.

'I will perform a sacrifice,' Senex announced. 'I will find something, never fear.'

CHAPTER 7

'So you're quite attached to the mutt, then?' old Senex said, nodding in the direction of Dog, who was standing nearby and looking up at the meat pie in the old man's hand hopefully.

Callie threw her arms protectively around the scrawny animal, causing a puff of dust and dried dung to rise into the air and unhoming a dozen fleas. Marcus narrowed his eyes, and centurion Gallo glanced at the pair and then back at Senex with an unmoving look.

'You are not sacrificing Dog. He's one of us now.'

Scriptor rolled his eyes. 'Besides, dogs aren't really sacrificial animals.'

'If it's made of meat, then it counts,' sniffed Senex, and everyone nodded sagely, because the old man held all the sacred secrets and performed all the religious rites for the unit.

As the others frowned – wondering where they could find any animal that wasn't either a friend or a giant, snapping killer reptile – Marcus pursed his lips in thought, his eyes dropping to the slavering, bright-eyed hopeful stray dog and then up to the current object of the animal's affections.

The meat pie.

He winced at the idea. Senex was over fifty summers old. No one knew exactly how old, of course – even Senex himself – but he was probably nearer sixty than fifty, and was by far the oldest man in the century, if not in the whole legion. And one of the consequences of his advanced age was the fact that his teeth had been abandoning him at an accelerated rate these past few years and he was clinging onto the last three like a falling man grabs at a branch.

While the men of the legion ate their hard salted meats and the hard-tack biscuits called *bucellatum* – which tasted like old socks but felt like boot-leather – Senex simply couldn't eat those foods anymore, for want of at least six more teeth.

And so, being an important man – the one who was closest to the gods – and something of a 'batty uncle' figure for the unit, a number of the men had taken pity on him and spent time when they prepared their own meals tenderising meat for him and making nice soft pies that were kind to his gums. It happened every noon and every night, and Senex's pies were precious to him.

Marcus sidled across to him. 'Senex?'

'Yes boy?'

'I suspect you're holding the answer.'

The old soldier blinked in surprise, and then sighed as he viewed the doomed pie in his hand. He'd been carefully holding it up out of the way of the dog for a while as they had talked, but now he was going to lose it anyway.

'If it's made of meat, it counts,' the old man repeated, weighing the pie in his hand and trying to ignore the rumbling in his stomach that he would not be satisfying any time soon.

Uncle Scriptor frowned. 'You don't mean…?'

'I mean the pie. Young Marcus is right. It counts.'

The standard bearer, his heavy burden propped against a ruined wall next to him, shook his head in disbelief. 'You are our *sacerdos* – our priest. You're the man who intercedes with the gods on our behalf and carries out all the sacred rites and rituals of the great and noble Roman state and its unconquered military. And you want to sacrifice a *meat pie*? Have you lost your mind, old man?'

Senex simply shrugged. 'Unless you can spare the mutt?'

Callie wrapped herself tighter round the filthy dog's neck as it continued to drool, its gaze following every movement of the meat pie. Marcus felt torn. His uncle clearly thought the idea mad, and Marcus should be emulating his uncle as much as possible if he were to ever take his place in the century, but if the alternative to the pie was Dog…

He looked across at the centurion, willing him to accept the idea.

Gallo looked down at Callie and her pet – the unit's new mascot – and then nodded at the old man. 'Senex knows what he's doing. If he says he can do it with a meat pie, then he can do it with a meat pie.'

'Well I can't stand around and watch the sacred rites of the legion performed on the old man's crusty dinner.'

'Yes you can. Come on.'

Senex gestured to the small campfire that two of the legionaries who had stayed with them had started among the ruins using sticks and dead palm leaves from around the sandy ground. At the centurion's nod, he began the '*lustratio*' – the sacred procession of the sacrifice, holding the meat pie reverentially out in front like the sacred item it had suddenly become. Scriptor shouldered the heavy standard again and rolled his eyes at the sight.

Dog followed the procession faithfully, his eyes glued to the pie, with Callie wrapped around him and Marcus close by. The old man stopped not far from the fire, the pie held on the palm of one hand, and reached to his belt, where he kept his small ritual knife. Removing it from the sheath, he lifted it above the tasty morsel, to the interest and amusement of the six men seated nearby. There would be no chance of ritually bathing before the ceremony, unless he felt like performing it from the inside of a crocodile.

'Great Jupiter, ancient Janus, divine Vesta, wise Minerva bless us with the bounty of your knowledge. We seek entry to

117

this resting place of ancient kings for the greater glory of Rome.'

With a deep breath, the old military priest plunged the knife down into the pie, somewhat slower and more carefully than was strictly called for, in order not to drive the point into his palm. As the blade passed between two fingers, the sweet, meaty juices dribbled across his hand and down the blade to drip and pool on the ground beneath him.

A couple of the legionaries snorted with laughter at the sight and Scriptor was giving the old man a look that clearly said *'you have lost your marbles'*, as the old man shook the pie to release as much of the juice as possible, and then prised it open with the knife to look inside.

'The organs are healthy,' he pronounced, at which Callie gave a light giggle.

'Healthy?' snorted Scriptor. 'They're a month old, salted, tenderised and cooked into a pie!'

Senex glared at the standard bearer before rummaging in the pie's interior. After a few long moments, he sighed and straightened.

'I can see nothing of use in the pie,' he announced. 'Should have eaten it after all,' he added quietly.

'Not a surprise,' grumbled Scriptor, 'you mad old man.'

Flashing another angry glance at the standard bearer, Senex turned and ritually – and with obvious regret in his eyes – cast the pie into the camp fire as an offering to the gods, where it sizzled and bubbled before beginning to blacken and burn.

'So much for that idiotic idea,' grumbled Scriptor.

Marcus frowned as he watched the sacrifice end. Something was nagging at him as the grown-ups argued, but he couldn't quite think what it was. He looked again at the sizzling charred pie. No. Not that. Nothing strange there. The other legionaries? No. He looked again at Senex, ignoring the ongoing arguments and insults. The man's hand was still raised, meat juices dripping from his fingertips. Dripping and falling to the dirty ground, creating small crowns of raised dust.

The ground…

With a grin of excitement, Marcus reached up and tugged at the trailing leopard skin that hung down his uncle's back from the helmet. Scriptor turned in surprise and, still grinning, Marcus pointed at the ground beneath the old priest.

'What?' muttered his uncle, irritably.

'It *worked*. Look!'

Scriptor, Senex and the centurion peered at the floor in the late afternoon sun. With a start of surprise, they too realised that the juice of the meat pie had almost gone, seeping down into the cracks between the stones.

119

'It must be hollow,' Marcus said excitedly. 'There *are* rooms underneath.'

'Not just that,' added Potens as he stopped making marks on his wax tablet and cupped his hand to his ear, 'but I would say it's an entrance of sorts. Listen.'

Marcus, moving above the stain, strained to pick out whatever Potens had heard, trying to block out the general sounds of the river and the trees.

'Shush!' Gallo barked at the half-dozen legionaries around the fire, who fell silent at the order. The only noises now were the gentle hiss of the air through the palm branches, Dog scratching his fleas, and a quiet whispered melody coming from the irrepressible Callie.

As they strained, they could just hear it.

The sound of dripping. The *spat, spat, spat* of liquid falling a long way and landing on a hard floor. It sounded echoey, as though in a cave. The meat juice had run between the slabs and was dripping onto the floor of the room below.

With a grin, Potens took his water-skin from his belt and tipped the precious, life-saving liquid onto the floor where the meat juices had pooled. The water quickly ran between the cracks, washing away more dust and making the narrow line clearly visible. The dripping sound suddenly sped up, echoing around the chamber beneath.

'Thank you, divine Minerva,' Marcus grinned, adding, 'and the others,' in case the rest of the gods took exception at being left out.

Potens turned to the silent, expectant legionaries around the fire and pointed at the two largest. 'Maximus? Brutus? Bring the tools.'

While the unit's biggest legionaries scurried off to their packs to collect shovels, picks and other tools, the engineer crouched, putting his wax tablet aside and using his bare hands to brush the sand and dust from the huge slab. Without being asked, Marcus and Callie dropped to help and by the time the legionaries had returned with their kit, the three of them had cleared off a huge rectangle of stone and revealed the deep crack that ran all the way around it. Now that it was clear, they could see that it had faint marks all along one edge – the hieroglyphic writing of the ancient Egyptians.

'Hey,' the centurion waved at the old seer who was sitting on a low, ruined wall, looking distinctly miserable again. The elderly native glance round, his face falling even further as he realised he was required again.

'Come and look at this,' Gallo shouted.

The seer strolled over and peered down at the slab.

'Very nice.'

'What do the words say?'

The seer crouched down and ran his finger along the lines of pictures.

'Bird, wavy line, semi-circle, bird, wobbly thing,' announced the old man as Callie frowned, trying to make sense of the writing.

'Very funny,' snapped the centurion. 'What does it all mean?'

Callie looked up, pointing at three of the symbols. 'That's the name Sobek. And I think this long one here is the name of the pharaoh in the pyramid.'

The seer grumbled as he read the lines. 'It's a warning not to enter the labyrinth. It is sacred to Amenemhat and to the crocodile god and if you go in, you'll bring a horrible curse down on us all.'

'Pretty much what I expected, then,' Gallo shrugged. 'Again I have to say I'm a lot more concerned about facing prefect Turbo empty handed than about the curse of an ancient Crocodile king.'

'Then you're an idiot,' the old Egyptian seer grumbled, scurrying off as the centurion glared at him. Potens was busy running his fingers all about the cracks at the edge, and Callie reached out and picked up the engineer's wax tablet where he had left it. Opening it, she ignored the wax sheet covered in her friend's spidery writing and used the pen to copy the hieroglyphs from the stone onto the clear side. Something else was familiar there, as well as the names of the god and the pharaoh.

'Come on,' Potens said, rubbing his dusty hands together and beckoning to the two legionaries, who wandered over with their tools. Callie stepped back with Marcus to allow the soldiers to do their work. Maximus furrowed his enormous, heavy brow as he hefted his pick and inserted the point in the narrow crack, close to the picture writing where Potens was pointing. Brutus flexed his arm muscles, making his Spanish bull tattoos ripple and dance, and followed suit, and a moment later the two men had their tools in position, their feet braced and waiting for the command.

The engineer turned and waited for the centurion's orders. Gallo threw up a quick prayer to Mars, the god of war, just in case Sobek's curse decided to eat them all, and then nodded at Potens.

The two big legionaries pushed down on the handles of their picks, grunting and heaving and straining. The weight of the great stone must be enormous, thought Marcus. He had once seen the two men pick up a fully-grown cow and move it out of the way of the supply wagons, and yet they struggled with this block. The huge stone rumbled and shuddered and the legionaries took a deep breath, clenched their teeth, and strained, the veins standing out on their arms and their foreheads.

After a moment of watching, Potens stepped across to his own kit pack and collected an identical pick, running across with it, inserting it into the crack between the two legionaries and lending his additional strength to the task. Though he was considerably smaller than the century's two giants, years of building things and digging holes had given the engineer good, strong, powerful muscles, and his extra weight tipped their effort over the edge, the stone lifting slightly with a heavy, grating noise.

As the slab rose enough to reveal an inch of darkness beneath, Potens, straining with the weight, nodded towards the children and then to his own kit lying nearby. 'If you would? The wedges?'

Marcus blinked for a moment and then saluted. He and Callie ran across to Potens' pack and dug around until they found two large wooden triangles that the engineer used to wedge carts' wheels on hills and stop them rolling back. Worrying about the safety of his fingers, Marcus shoved his wedge into the gap under the lifted stone at one side while Callie inserted the other. Once the children had stepped back, the three men let their tools go loose and allowed the wedges to take the weight of the stone, pausing to rub their muscles and suck in deep breaths.

'Phew. That's heavy,' panted Potens, and even Maximus and Brutus nodded, their eyes wide.

'There must have been other ways in.' Scriptor mused, and Potens nodded. 'I think so. This is a one-use entrance. I suspect when they first built the structure, they had a few places like this where they needed a big hole to lower large things into the underground. But once those things were inside they could seal it up and not use it again.'

'Are you ready?' the engineer asked as he looked at his two accomplices. Maximus and Brutus nodded and the three men bent to the task again, shoving the picks deeper into the crack and heaving. As the stone rose again, slightly easier this time, the engineer removed his tool, moved around the side, and then inserted it again, using the angle to help ease the enormous stone across sideways.

After a few moments of puffing and panting, the three men managed to shift the stone to one side, revealing a wide, black hole.

'Good work,' Gallo nodded, running across to the fire, picking up one of the larger branches and lifting it so that the burning end glowed in the orange light of late afternoon.

Carrying it back to the hole, he leaned over and, taking a deep breath, dropped the torch into the hole.

The burning branch fell into the darkness and Marcus felt his heart thump in shock as he reared back at the sight of the huge green crocodile head, before the torch hit the floor and went out, returning the hole to darkness.

It took a moment for him to realise the crocodile-headed man had been a painting on a wall below. He heaved in a deep breath as the centurion smiled.

'Let's get some light down there.'

CHAPTER 8

Callie's journal

Diadorus Siculus said of this labyrinth that it was ingenious. That 'a man who enters it cannot easily find his way out'. Herodotus said that 'at the corner where the labyrinth ends there is, nearby, a pyramid 240 feet high and engraved with great animals. The road to this is made underground.' This suggests a difficult time ahead, but it does seem to bear out that the labyrinth would be the best way to gain access to the pyramid. Like all good students, I must take the ancient writers with a pinch of salt. After all, Strabo said the labyrinth had only one floor, while Herodotus claims two. But then, perhaps Strabo discounted the top floor because only the bottom one was a maze.

And given that Strabo says the pyramid is four hundred feet along each side, while my own measurements make it nearer three hundred, we can only rely on what we find with our own hands and see with our own eyes.

The centurion will not want us to go inside. Marcus seems oblivious to the fact. But I need to see the inside. I will find a way. Even if the inside is dangerous and creepy, there are crocodiles out here, and dark is not too far off.

Mark my words. I will see inside the labyrinth.

Marcus watched as Maximus and Brutus readied themselves, bracing their feet and lowering the ropes they held into the room below. Good bright-burning torches had been dropped into the darkness and the cellar-like chamber was now well lit, its floor some twenty feet below them. The walls were painted in bright colours, covered with pictures and hieroglyphics, a lot of it revolving around crocodiles. Callie squinted down with undisguised interest.

They could see at least three doorways leading off, and possibly another just at the edge of the lit area.

Gallo gestured to the two huge legionaries. 'Once we're down, you two need to drive some iron pegs into the ground and tie off the ropes so that we can get back out easily.'

'Is it a good idea to go in now, sir?' Marcus asked quietly. 'It's late in the day. We could wait until morning?'

The centurion shook his head. 'We have an hour or more of light left yet today, and I want to get as much done as fast as we can. The sooner we finish here and get back to Alexandria, the better for all of us.'

The two big legionaries nodded their understanding, unable to salute while they held the ropes ready to lower the adventurers down into the labyrinth. Four men would go in, Gallo had decided. Himself, obviously, since he was in charge. Senex, because the old man was the most knowledgeable about gods – even those of the Egyptians. Scriptor, because he had read about the place and knew more than anyone else, apart from Callie of course. And Potens the engineer, for his knowledge of buildings and tunnels and his practical mind. The other six legionaries and the old seer would wait at the top with Marcus and Callie, guarding the entrance until they returned.

Marcus was glowering and sulking at the order to stay behind on the surface. He'd argued that there were crocs out here, but Gallo had still said no. Callie was equally disappointed, though she was more interested in reading the walls than exploring the tunnels, and could see quite a bit from the entrance, where she lay with Potens' spare tablet, trying to identify which picture made which sound.

'We need to be extremely careful down here,' Scriptor said quietly. 'A labyrinth is, quite literally, a maze. We could very easily get lost. We must stay within sight of each other at all times.'

'We should drag a line in the dust, so that we can follow it back out,' old Senex suggested.

'Not good enough,' Scriptor replied. 'If we have to go back across our own path it will get so complicated we cannot work it out. Besides, if there is a heavy gust of wind, it could blow the line flat again.' He tapped his lip.

'Theseus,' said Marcus.

'What?'

'Do you know the tale of Theseus and the Minotaur? It's one of my favourite stories.'

Most of the others shook their heads. Few of the legionaries and their officers had much time for stories, though Scriptor grinned. 'Of course. Your father and I used to love that one as kids, too. Theseus had to find his way out of the Minotaur's labyrinth. He used a ball of twine as he explored, so he could follow it back out.'

'We haven't got any twine,' Potens murmured.

'We've got Porcus,' the centurion smiled, and gestured to one of the legionaries over by the fire. The man rose at Gallo's pointing and wandered across. Porcus was the portliest of the men in the century, officially far too overweight for the army, really, but better than anyone else at positioning and aiming the catapult, so he was given a lot of leeway and looked after despite his shape. And because of his large frame, his tunics had to be made to order by a tailor in Alexandria, and were of good quality knitted wool – a skill the Egyptians excelled at. He also always carried a spare with him, as he tended to get sweaty quite quickly.

'Porcus, you're joining us, and fetch your spare tunic, too,' the centurion smiled.

'Sir?'

131

'I'll see you get paid back for it, but it's needed for the good of the unit, Porcus.'

Unhappily, the rounded legionary retrieved his spare large, red tunic from his pack and carried it across to the entrance. Brutus and Maximus shared a worried look as they anchored the tops of the ropes with which they would now be lowering the huge Porcus. As the portly legionary tucked his spare clothing into his belt Scriptor bent, found the end of the wool on the man's tunic and unpicked it, grinning, as he turned the garment into a source of twine that he could use to mark their trail just as the Greek Theseus had done. Nodding, he handed the loose end to Brutus.

'Tie this to something so we can find our way back here.'

Once the legionary had fastened the loose end to the heavy rope he braced himself again. Gallo grasped the line and clenched his teeth, lowering himself into the darkness and then hand-over-hand climbing down the rope into the room below. Scriptor did the same with Maximus' rope, and when the two were safely inside, Senex and Potens came down, the old man managing without too much of a struggle.

Marcus strolled unhappily over to the hole and looked down at the four men gazing around themselves at the painted walls. He watched them remove their own torches as, with a groan, Porcus began to lower himself behind them. Each man carried three more of the flammable, pitch-soaked lights in their belt and, touching the first to the other ones on the floor, they flared into life.

'Ready?' Gallo asked as Porcus landed, and the others nodded, looking nervously around the room.

'Which doorway?' Scriptor asked.

'That one.'

'Why that one?'

'Because,' the centurion replied quietly, 'all the others are close to big crocodile paintings, and that one isn't!' The men began to move across the room, leaving a trail of red wool that rose to the hatch above.

A sudden explosion of barking filled the quiet, serene evening air, and Marcus turned to see dog running straight at him and Callie. In panic, he pushed her away and rolled to the side, trying not to fall into the hole, and dog hurtled past him, leaping into the hole and landing with surprising ease below, given how far down the drop was.

With a yelp, Callie suddenly lunged for the hole, her tablet discarded, grabbing the rope hanging from Maximus' hands and sliding down into the chamber so fast she felt her hands burning. As Gallo stopped and turned to shout at the girl, Marcus quickly hand-over-handed himself down after her.

'This is no place for you two.'

'I'm not leaving Dog,' grumbled Callie, patting the dusty head and folding her arms defiantly. Marcus walked across to her. 'Cal, we should go back up.'

The centurion nodded, but Callie simply narrowed her eyes in refusal and tightened her folded arms.

'Your niece needs to learn her place,' Gallo grumbled at Scriptor, and then looked across at Marcus. 'And you should know better. If you want to join up when you're old enough, you need to learn to obey orders.'

Marcus felt a cold shock of panic. Had he just crippled his chances? He saw Dog nuzzling the floor and scoffing something gleefully, as the grown-ups talked, and a suspicion grew in him.

'He was just looking after his sister, sir,' their uncle shrugged. 'What could be more in the spirit of the unit than that?'

'The two of you, take that mutt back up,' Gallo grunted.

'Erm… how?' replied Callie cheekily, and Uncle Scriptor grinned. 'That might be a difficult job. Besides, I feel happier with the animal with us. Dogs can see well in the dark, after all.'

The centurion glared at his standard bearer, then shifted that look to Callie, and finally back to Uncle Scriptor. 'Alright, but they stay at the back, keep with us, and promise not to get in the way.'

The standard bearer nodded and turned to the pair. 'Callie, you look after Dog. Marcus, you look after Callie. Understand?'

The two nodded, and Scriptor straightened again and readied himself to go. With a clearing of his throat, Potens turned and pointed across the room. 'I think we should go that way, sir.'

Gallo frowned. 'Why?'

'Because that's north, towards the pyramid. I don't know what we're expecting to find down here, sir, but unless anyone has a better idea, I'd say we ought to be working our way towards the pyramid, since that's where we want to end up.'

Gallo paused for a moment and then nodded. 'I suppose you're right. Come on, then.'

At the back, Marcus looked down at the marks in the dusty floor where Dog had been eating. His suspicion growing, he grabbed Callie's hand and sniffed.

'Spiced meat,' he whispered. 'That's why dog jumped in. You tricked him into it by waving spiced meat at him.'

Callie grinned. 'Got us inside, didn't it?'

Marcus stared at her for a moment, astonished. 'You nearly got us into a lot of trouble.'

'Nearly is a long way from actually,' Callie laughed. 'Come on. Let's find what we need.'

Flaring torches held aloft, the four soldiers crossed the room and made for the doorway opposite that Potens had indicated, Dog and the two children bringing up the rear. With a deep breath, they entered the corridor, which was several inches deep in dust and sand, both walls and ceiling painted with images of men, gods, vultures, and the hieroglyphics that seemed to be everywhere in this land. The cluttered images were almost enough to give a person a headache, and make them picture-blind, and the grown-ups tried to concentrate on the corridor and ignore the paintings around it, though Callie continued to examine them closely as she passed, picking out the odd symbols she recognised from other places and sounding out the letters she felt she knew. It was starting to fall into place as easily as Latin and Greek now she had found a few key symbols.

For a while Gallo led the group along the corridors, turning this way and that whenever he hit a junction, keeping his course steadily north, although it wasn't long before Marcus' sense of direction completely failed and he had no idea what way he was pointing any more. A brief consultation among the grown-ups led to the conclusion that they had drifted off-course some way. With a new sense of purpose, they forged ahead once more towards what Potens claimed was north. As if scared by the numerous dark openings of the side corridors they passed, Dog stayed close to Marcus and Callie at all times, the three bringing up the rear and staying as close as they could to the torchlight cast by the party of adults. In front of the children Porcus wobbled along, almost filling the corridor, the spare tunic unravelling continually and threading off past them and back into the darkness. His garment was fast running out and he looked distinctly unhappy.

Here and there in the seemingly-endless sequence of corridors, corners and junctions, they came across rooms, though what those chambers' original purposes had been they could not guess, since they were now all empty and deserted, covered in dust and paintings but lacking anything else.

After perhaps quarter of an hour of exploring, they had to pause for a moment while Porcus, his face a picture of misery, watched his last tunic thread unravel and, at Gallo's order, unpicked the low hem of the one he was wearing and tied it to the one that had already run out. Then they were off again, moving along the passages, turnings, junctions and through empty rooms, Porcus' remaining tunic beginning to unwind.

The tense, dim silence of the maze was broken suddenly by a burst of laughter. Marcus stared at Callie, who was giggling uncontrollably, and the other soldiers turned to look at them, Gallo's expression irritated.

'Sorry,' the girl chortled between breaths, and pointed at Porcus in front. The poor legionary's big tunic had unravelled enough that everyone could see the tops of his legs and the non-regulation pink underwear.

Porcus flushed the same colour as his underwear. 'Washed them with my tunic, sir. They went pink.'

Gallo rolled his eyes and shook his head as he led the party on into the darkness, made less oppressive by Porcus' glowing face. Finally, almost half an hour into their travels, the portly legionary pleaded for them to stop.

'What's up?' Gallo asked wearily, looking back at the almost-naked legionary, who was now attired only in his pink underwear and a thin necklace of red wool – all that was left of his tunic.

'We've only got a few feet left, sir. Then we're stuck.'

Gallo nodded dejectedly. 'Time to go back.'

'We could just try a different direction, sir?' Marcus prompted from the rear.

'Not really, lad. We've not got much more than half an hour of light left upstairs and these torches won't last much longer. I'm already on my second. We'll have to get more wool and try again in the morning.

'Can we just try a few feet further sir?' Callie asked quietly from the back.

'What?'

'Just another corner or two. I smell books.'

'No one can *smell* books,' Senex scoffed.

'Shows how much you know you, you old fool,' Scriptor grinned. '*Callie* can smell dusty papyrus. If she says there are books here somewhere, then there are.'

Callie shuffled with difficulty past the pale, sweaty naked form of Porcus. 'He's right, sir. There *are* books here. I can *feel* them.' Marcus nodded encouragingly. His sister had an uncanny ability to locate literature.

Gallo frowned. 'We've not got much wool left. It's dangerous.' He paused for a moment and then reluctantly nodded. 'Scriptor? You, Senex and young Callie here go ahead two more corners, then. The rest of us will stay here. No further than that, mind,' he added. 'I don't want to have to bring all the men down here to search for you.'

Tensely, with a feeling of building nervousness, Marcus watched the three figures disappear off around the corner and waited, sensing a similar worry from the engineer nearby. He knew that Potens was as fond of the girl as her uncle was, and the engineer looked unhappy to see Callie going off into the dark, even with the standard bearer. He felt a wrench himself.

What if they were walking into danger? He would never be able to live with himself if he failed to protect her as he'd promised. He began to try and edge around Porcus.

'What do we do if they…' Potens began.

'They will be back in a moment,' Gallo said firmly.

'I hope so, because…'

He was interrupted by a shout.

'Come on, sir!' called Scriptor from around the corner ahead, and the excitement and lack of panic in his voice soothed Marcus as he dropped back behind Porcus again. The centurion and the engineer looked at each other, shrugged, and then set off ahead. As he took his fifth step forward, the very last of Porcus' tunic unravelled and the legionary dropped the wool thread as it reached its limit. With no other option, Marcus, at the rear, pulled out his sword and used it like a rudder, dragging it deep through the dust and sand to create a furrow that should lead them back to the end of the wool. Then he hurried on to keep up.

'Where are you?' Gallo shouted irritably. 'Keep talking so we can find you.'

As Callie began to sing her favourite song about the thin hippo and the fat ibis, they followed her voice around several corners and past a junction, Marcus still dragging his sword to leave a trail, until they spotted a doorway that glowed with the light of the two men's torches.

Entering, Gallo was already snapping angrily at them. 'I told you: *two* corners and no more. You idiots, you could have…' His voice trailed off into silence as he looked around the room. Marcus emerged into the chamber blinking with surprise. Callie *had* been right about being able to smell books. Unlike every other room they had found, which had been empty and dusty, this one was *filled* with books. Every wall, instead of being decorated with paintings and inscriptions, was covered with wooden racks that held hundreds of papyrus scrolls, all neatly rolled up.

'That's impressive. It's like a library.'

'It *is* a library,' Callie replied happily, clambering along the racks as her uncle did the same in the other direction.

'Can you find anything useful?' Marcus asked hopefully, finding it hard to believe they had come across the place at all.

'It's a problem,' Scriptor replied, rubbing his temple with two fingers. 'These are really old. Long before the locals knew Latin, and even before they spoke Greek. All the books in here are in hieroglyphics. Very old. I can read Latin and Callie knows Greek, but none of us have got to grips with ancient Egyptian. I know a few words and can piece bits together, but not enough to read properly.'

Callie nodded her agreement. 'I can make out what might be a few short phrases, and might be able to pick out something useful, but this is complicated.'

'Lucky we've got a man upstairs who speaks it like a native then, eh?' Gallo grinned, picturing the miserable old seer sitting grumpily and waiting as the sun sank in the west.

'Let's just have a little look around anyway, sir, before we go.'

Marcus nodded. It would be daft to have come all this way and not spend a little time checking around, after all. He peered up encouragingly at the centurion, who caught his look and sighed. 'Go on, then. Not long, though.'

As Gallo and the others stood in the doorway, occasionally glancing back out to make sure that the line Marcus had dragged in the sand was still there to lead them back, Scriptor and Callie pored over the shelves, old Senex and Marcus scurrying over to lend a hand.

As the four searched a wall each for anything that might be of interest, Marcus perused the shelves, trying to note anything odd. He read Latin well enough, but this language was so far beyond him, he stood no chance of actually reading them, so all he could do was see if anything stood out in some way. In his experience Fortuna, the goddess of luck, could be every bit as useful as a little learning. Something caught his eye and he moved over to an area of bare shelving.

'This is interesting,' he said from the corner in the dimmest of light.

'What is?' asked Gallo and Scriptor at the same time, stepping towards him and holding the torches high to help illuminate the area.

'There's a whole section missing here, I think, sir.' *Thank you, Fortuna*, he grinned.

The group moved to that part of the room and peered at the shelving. In the improved light, he could see that some two dozen or more recesses in the rack were empty, their scrolls gone.

'I wonder what they were, and why they were removed?' Potens mused.

'I don't know, sir,' Marcus replied, 'but it wasn't that long ago. Look.'

As the other three frowned, he ran his finger along the ancient wood of the scroll rack, leaving a faint line in the fine layer of white. 'See? Hardly any dust. All the other racks and the scrolls are thick with dust they've been here so long. Not this, though. These scrolls were taken away quite recently.'

'Someone else has been here then?' the centurion mused.

'Yes.'

143

As Gallo and Potens pondered the problem, the others going back to their perusing of the racks, Dog sat in the middle of the floor and began to scratch behind his ear, sending up small clouds of dust.

'Think I've got something too,' Callie said excitedly.

The other three rushed across to her, leaving Dog to excavate his fleas in peace.

'What is it?' Marcus asked eagerly. It was unlike him to get excited in a library, but this was different. This was not a lesson but an adventure, and any advance here might take them closer to the pyramid and its gold.

Callie unrolled her current scroll against the shelves and displayed it to them. Marcus frowned as he peered at it. 'Looks the same as all the rest to me; just lots of Egyptian writing.'

'Not quite, brother. Look closely. Here.'

She pointed at the scroll, tapping her finger on a particular point. Centurion Gallo leaned down next to Marcus, squinting in the bad light, and a smile crossed his face slowly.

'Is that a map?'

'Something like that, sir,' Callie grinned. 'It's a bit rough, but that square has to be the pyramid and this big rectangle has to be the maze, because it shows the canal running past. And this triangle hieroglyph here means pyramid. I've seen it before, in the library back in Alexandria and on the stone we moved to get in here.'

'Then that means…'

'Yes!' barked Uncle Scriptor excitedly, leaping forward and almost knocking Marcus down. 'This little mark here on the square must be the entrance to the pyramid. And it's not in the north as is usually the case. Potens and the lads could have spent a month removing the stones on the north side and they would never have found it because it's in the *south*, facing the labyrinth.'

Gallo smiled. 'Let's take this scroll out. The old seer can translate the rest of it for us. Was there anything else useful there with it?'

'No sir,' Callie shrugged. 'But it doesn't seem to be the same sort of scroll as the others around it. They're all marked with sort if 'U' shape, which I think means something to do with ghosts, but this one is labelled with the triangle of the pyramid. I think it had been put back in the wrong place.'

Marcus grinned. 'I bet it should have been with the ones that have already been taken away, looking at the shape and size of the holes in the rack.'

Gallo stretched his arms. 'Something about that bothers me, but now it's time we got out of here. It'll be dark outside soon.

And now we have a lead, so in the morning we can start looking for the entrance.'

The others smiled and nodded. With Scriptor holding tightly onto the scroll, the party turned and strode back out of the room. Sighing with relief, Marcus found that his dust trail remained and he could find his way back to the end of the wool, and he almost sagged as he gripped the red line and began to wind it around his hand as they retraced the trail. Gallo's second torch burned out a few moments later and rather than light the third, he took the wool from Marcus and continued to wind, gesturing for him to shuffle to the back as before.

Slowly and carefully, they made their way back through the labyrinth, heading for their entrance, Gallo now leading the way with Potens, Senex and Porcus behind him, followed by Scriptor and then the children bringing up the rear. It was strange and eerie, moving in silence and dim light, but no one seemed to wish to break that quiet, and they slowly made their way back.

Marcus almost jumped out of his skin as Potens ahead suddenly said: 'Did you hear that, sir?'

'Good gods, man,' the centurion snapped. 'Don't do that. You nearly stopped my heart.'

Marcus nodded emphatically, his own heart racing. Everyone seemed shaken by the sudden breaking of the silence, even Callie, who had gone pale by his side. The column came to a halt and Potens said again. 'But *listen*, sir.'

All of them kept silent, the only noise the crackling and guttering of the flaming torches and the slobbering of Dog. Then suddenly they all heard it: a shuffling, scraping noise off in the dark ahead.

'What is it?' Callie asked in a whisper.

'I have no idea,' hissed Marcus in reply.

'I'm not sure I want to find out, either,' added the centurion from ahead.

The engineer's torch behind the centurion was raised high, and Marcus crouched and peered down the corridor past and between the legs of the soldiers. A few paces ahead there was a crossroads, with passages running off left and right. Ahead, all was darkness.

'I can't tell where it's coming from, but it's *somewhere* up ahead,' hissed Potens.

Gallo nodded. 'I can't see which direction the wool goes in from here either.' With a deep breath, the centurion held up his free hand. 'Hang on. I'm going to tug the wool so we can see it stretching off ahead. Keep that torch raised and everyone watch carefully.'

Lifting his hand, Gallo began to wind in the slack of the wool round his hand.

'Something's wrong,' he said quietly.

'What?' Marcus breathed, the first strains of panic beginning to grip him.

'The wool has been at full stretch all the way, and I've kept it taut all the way back, but now there's loads of slack to wind in.'

'You don't mean…?' Uncle Scriptor murmured.

Gallo nodded as the group's worst fear came true and the snapped end of the red wool suddenly sprang up from the floor.

'I can't have pulled it tight enough to snap it,' he frowned.

Potens looked past him at the end of wool he held up into the light. 'No, sir. Look at it. A square end to the strand. It's been cut, not broken. Someone did it deliberately!'

'Uh oh,' was all Marcus could find to say as he realised they were less than half way back and with no way to work out even where the other end of the wool was, let alone the entrance.

'We might be able to follow our own footprints,' Callie hazarded, looking doubtfully at the faint scuff marks on the floor all around them.

A little way ahead, Uncle Scriptor cleared his throat. 'Can I remind you,' he hissed, 'that there is more to think about than snapped wool!'

Remembering what had made them stop in the first place, the men fell silent again. The shuffling and scraping was a lot louder now. 'What do we do?' whispered Marcus, clenching his bladder and trying to keep the waver of fear out of his voice.

'We have to go forward anyway,' Gallo replied. 'We need to try and follow our own footprints back out. It means we'll have to go slowly, but there's not much we can do about that.'

Slowly, quietly, the group moved forward, almost creeping along the passageway, each of them tense and worried. Pace by pace, they approached the crossroads.

'I think our footprints go straight ahead,' the centurion hissed, 'but I can't be absolutely sure until we get there.'

'That noise is getting louder,' Marcus said, his voice now definitely wavering.

'No it isn't!' replied Potens sharply, and the explorers stopped moving and held their breath. In fact there was now no sound at all apart from the flickering of the torches and the ever-present smelly breath of Dog.

'I don't know about you,' their uncle muttered, 'but I find the fact that it's stopped a lot more worrying than the sound was.'

'You are soldiers of Rome,' Gallo snapped, 'who have fought battles and rebellions, and trained to be the best warriors in the world. If I have to tell the prefect that my men shiver at a noise in a tunnel, I will be the most embarrassed centurion in the army's history. Pull yourselves together.'

But even from the back, where Marcus was on the verge of panic, he could see that Gallo was trembling slightly. It made him feel a little better about how un-soldierly he was feeling right now.

'Come on,' the centurion sighed. 'Let's follow our footsteps.'

The party moved forward towards the crossroads and, just to add to their nerves, the torch Potens held above his commander's shoulder suddenly went out, plunging the corridor into even deeper gloom. Grumbling, Gallo whipped his third torch from his belt and turned, passing it to the engineer.

'Here. Light this.'

Potens touched the pitch-soaked stick to one of the others further back and it burst into flame. With a sense of profound relief, Marcus saw the light levels in the eerie corridor rise.

Smiling, Centurion Gallo turned to them all, pointing at the tracks in the floor ahead.

'It looks like we...' As the centurion turned, his eyes swept past the side passage and his face paled. 'Run!' he shouted with a yelp.

Marcus felt the panic return, and this time it brought a whole gang of friends. He ran with the rest, Callie at his side and Dog behind, almost snapping at their heels. As they passed the crossroads, his eyes swivelled to the dark hallway and he caught a brief flash of what had made the centurion run. Callie had also seen and gave a squeak of uncharacteristic fear, which frightened Marcus more even than the thing he'd seen. Very little unsettled his sister. His blood froze and his legs pushed for extra speed as he realised he was at the back with Callie and Dog and all the soldiers were up front.

His uncle seemed to have had the same thought for, as he passed into the corridor ahead, Scriptor flattened himself against the wall to let Marcus and Callie run past, and then drew his sword before breaking into a run again and following them, bringing up the rear protectively.

Gallo was already halfway to the next corner in the corridor before the others caught up with him, their faces as white as his. Glancing back over his shoulder, past his uncle, Marcus saw the creature round the corner, following them with a jerky, slow pace. Its face was that of the crocodile god, with gleaming yellow eyes in a scaly green head, jutting white fangs to either side of the snout and steam rising from the nostrils. The body wore the white pleated skirt of the Egyptian priests and gods and the elaborate gold and jewelled collar they favoured. But it was not flesh, that body. It was dusty brown stone, cracking at the elbows and knees as it moved.

'How do we get out?' yelled Scriptor from the back, as he prepared to fight off the monster, his voice betraying a level of dread Marcus had never before heard from the brave standard bearer.

'I don't know,' Gallo replied breathlessly from the front.

Before anyone else could chip in, Dog barked loudly and pushed past their legs, racing off into the darkness ahead, yapping as he went.

'Follow Dog!' Marcus yelled, and the short column of men began to run again, his feet pounding in pursuit of the animal that could be their saviour. It was a tremendous relief as they rounded a corner and lost sight of the monster god-guardian behind them, and an even *greater* relief when they found the severed end of the red wool on the floor ahead, where the trail started once more.

But they didn't need the wool line. Ignoring the trail, they pounded along in the wake of Dog, who barked enthusiastically

152

as he ran ahead, and soon, with sighs of relief all round, they spotted the dim glow of a room lit by the setting sun and the thin brown lines of the two ropes hanging down.

'Thank you, Fortuna,' Marcus said as they ran out into the chamber and he and Callie were pushed forward to grab the ropes and haul themselves back out of these monster-infested tunnels.

CHAPTER 9

His hands tired from climbing the rope, Marcus' head rose above ground level once again into the gloom of the evening. The sun had now vanished behind the western hills and only the orange-purple glow of evening remained. The searing heat of the Egyptian day had given way to the stuffy warmth of the Egyptian night.

There was no sign of Maximus or Brutus, but that was not surprising. The centurion had told them to anchor the ropes to iron spikes in the ground and they had done just that and then gone off on their own business, probably for food and to rest their giant aching muscles after all their hard work.

Behind him, on the other side of the square hole, Callie clambered, shaking and pale, up onto the dirt and as Marcus moved aside to make room for Gallo right behind him, Uncle Scriptor followed his sister up at the far side, collapsing to the ground and panting with relief. Marcus had never seen his uncle truly frightened before but, following on in the wake of a few days of crocodile-orientated trouble, coming face-to-face with the crocodile god himself had drained all the colour from the standard bearer's face. Even Callie had been unusually silent and clingy on their way out.

With a sigh, Marcus rolled away from the edge. Moments later first Potens and then old Senex appeared at the top of the ropes and pulled themselves out onto the dirt.

With a smile, recovering himself, Gallo spat on his hands to improve his grip, and then began hauling the rope up from the darkness below. Slowly the shape of Dog appeared in the gloom, carefully tied to the end of the rope with it looped twice beneath him to make a stable and comfortable ride. Dog arrived panting at the top and as the centurion began to untie the ropes from around him, licked the man's dusty face with gratitude.

'I would say he's earned two square meals a day now, eh lads?' Gallo grinned. 'We'd have been in real trouble down there without him.'

The others went quiet at that thought and the memory of the crocodile-headed god-statue-guardian thing that had loomed out of the darkness at them. Across the way, Scriptor and Potens helped haul the almost-naked form of Porcus up to the surface.

It took a few heartbeats for the weary explorers to notice the noise in the background of their silence, but a moment later they were all on their feet. Every one of them, both soldier and civilian, recognised the sound of battle after years of the rebellion that had swept through the east of the Empire and the riot that had ruined their city, and the noises they could hear from the slope were the unmistakable sounds of men forming a line with their shields raised and clonking against each other.

The commotion was overridden by the distant sound of Brutus calling for them to 'stay steady' and 'hold the line'.

'Come on!' Gallo shouted.

The seven of them ran off towards the commotion, the grown-ups drawing their swords as they ran, passing the now low-burning campfire and reaching the edge of the wide plateau formed by the ruins on the labyrinth's roof.

In surprise, they drew themselves up sharply. The half-dozen men who had remained above the maze waiting for the explorers were down the slope a little way, formed into a short line with their shields slammed together into a wall of painted wood, their glinting swords just visible.

But they were not facing barbarians. Nor were they defending themselves against Judean rebels, or even bandits or rioters. The shapes of a dozen large crocs were lined up before them like a swaying, crawling army of teeth and scales. The beasts were clearly intent on getting at the legionaries, and the soldiers were holding them off, but were clearly in trouble. Each time one of the large reptiles decided to have a go, stamping forward and opening and closing its jaws with a snap that was audible even up here, they were frustrated by the shields of the legionaries, which were kept in a solid wall and slammed on the ground to prevent bites beneath them. But because no man was willing to move his shield and open himself to one of those unpleasant snaggle-toothed snouts, the soldiers could not reach to jab at the crocs with their swords.

Not that that would be much use. The Roman short swords were the perfect weapon for fighting a normal battle, but against these things what they really needed was a long spear that would keep them safely out of the way of the teeth.

'What do we do?' Potens asked breathlessly as they watched the strange stand-off.

'We could go and rouse the rest of the men on the other side of the pyramid?' Senex suggested. 'With eighty men we could do it.'

'Fire!' said Marcus, snapping his fingers.

'Boy?' the centurion frowned at him.

'All animals are afraid of fire, sir. I see no reason why crocodiles will be any different.'

Gallo nodded with a grim smile. 'Come on,' he said.

As they made to run, the centurion paused and turned with a raised hand. 'Not you two. Not this time. You stay up here and out of trouble.' Marcus, who had drawn his wooden sword, felt his lip wobble a little at the command. He could be of use...

But their uncle appeared at the centurion's side and nodded his agreement, pointing at the plateau firmly. Defeated, Callie and Marcus dropped to a crouch to watch.

With the others hot on his heels, Gallo ran over to the campfire, which had not been tended for some time. Selecting one of the larger logs, he lifted it so that the glowing orange end rose from the fire, spitting and then bursting into renewed flame. His four companions followed suit and a moment later the five men were running down the hillside towards the crocodiles, waving the burning torches.

Marcus reached out to stroke Dog as he watched, only to discover that the animal wasn't there. He glanced around, and saw the mutt beyond the camp fire, out of the way. Pursing his lips he turned back to watch the action below.

Gallo had reacted instantly, knowing that his men were in danger, and as the soldiers closed on the monsters, the crocs were showing no sign of fear at the five flaming logs being waved at them. In fact, one of them seemed to be grinning as he watched the men running at him, like a meal delivering itself into his mouth.

Watching from the labyrinth roof, Marcus uttered a prayer to Fortuna as the centurion reached the fight, waving the branch at the big, grinning crocodile and shouting at it, calling it names and demanding that it run away. Gallo hissed loudly, and for a long moment Marcus actually thought that the beast was simply going to snap those enormous jaws at him and bite off his arm, swallowing both it and the torch it held.

But then the creature took a step back.

Feeling a flood of relief at the sight, Marcus watched the centurion take a tentative step forward, waving the flaming log and jabbing it towards the monster. He tried to imagine being there himself. Gripping his shield tight and thrusting a blade, helping Gallo fight off the crocodiles. He swished his wooden sword through the air a few times and watched, wishing he was a little bit older. Callie, nearby, was still pale and quiet, her eyes locked on the beasts below, silent.

As more of the crocs had turned towards the fire-wielding soldiers, Maximus and Brutus had taken the opportunity to move their shields aside for a brief moment and use their swords to jab at the creatures. Their attacks wouldn't go through the heavy, armoured hides, and all they did was annoy the crocs into turning back at them, so the two giant legionaries moved behind the safety of their shields again.

But now, subjected to undignified prodding at one side and angry fire at the other, the crocs seemed to lose interest in what had previously looked like an easy meal and began to turn and waddle away down the slope towards the canal. The five adventurers continued to wave their burning logs until the last of the beasts had retreated, and did not lower the weapons until the things were down at the water's edge and slumping into the wet mud, watching the Romans irritably, like a naughty child told to go to bed early.

'Thanks, sir,' Maximus rumbled, breaking up the shield-wall and sheathing his sword with relief. 'I was starting to think we were in real trouble there.'

'You *were* in real trouble,' Scriptor replied, shivering. Assuming the fight to be over and therefore the centurion's orders to have been complied with, Marcus and Callie rose and began to plod down the slope to the soldiers, Marcus eagerly, Callie nervously.

'What happened?' Gallo asked his men as the children approached. He dropped his branch and let it sputter and go out in the sand and dust.

'Don't know, sir,' Brutus replied, strolling over. 'Can't explain it. We were just sorting out some more food and trying to make Senex a new pie when suddenly the lad on watch started shouting. By the time he got up to us and we all had our helmets on and shields up, the things were already up the slope and moving to attack. What brought them here so suddenly I don't know, but they came in force.'

'Yes, I saw that.'

'Where's the dog?' asked Potens, looking around.

'He doesn't like crocodiles any more than Secundus does,' the centurion waved his arm towards the labyrinth. 'I expect he's hiding back up in the ruins. I wouldn't blame him.'

Marcus' gaze scoured the area for their pet as he approached and started as he spotted the mangy stray in an unexpected place. 'I don't know, sir,' he said to the centurion in a nervous voice, pointing down the slope. 'For a dog who doesn't like crocs, he's getting awfully close to them!'

They turned to see Dog wandering across the slope, halfway down to the canal and its deadly denizens, snuffling around.

'Dog!' Callie yelled in a quavering voice, worried that one of the crocodiles might spot the stray and consider it an easy meal for the taking after the armoured men they had tried and been thwarted by. Far from coming at the shout, the dog ignored the call and continued snuffling around on the sandy slope.

'Dog!' Gallo repeated. 'Come here, Dog!'

Still the stray paid no attention.

'What's got into him?'

Marcus frowned. 'I don't know, but there's some more of it getting into him now.'

They watched in incomprehension as Dog nuzzled something on the ground, pawed at it a little, turning it over, and then began to wolf it down hungrily.

'It could be *anything*,' his uncle muttered. 'That dog would eat a *rock* if you dusted it with flour.'

'Whatever it is, he's enjoying it,' Marcus noted.

'You'd better go get him,' Gallo muttered. 'If we don't, one of the crocs will.'

Uncle Scriptor nodded and, with Marcus and Callie at his heel, walked steadily down the slope, slowing as he closed on the dog and the canal beyond. 'Stay back you two. If one of those crocs starts to come out of the water, you run up the beach and get behind Brutus and Maximus.' Marcus nodded his understanding and then stopped as his wandering gaze spotted something unusual.

Shuffling across the sand, he crouched down. The dirt was stained pinky-red at his feet, though in the evening gloom he'd not noticed it until he was almost above it. Frowning, he stood and peered around. Sure enough he could see, as well as the tracks and drag-marks from the crocodiles going up and down the slope, and the paw prints of Dog, another few pink stains dotted up and down. Callie approached another and crouched to examine it, as did their uncle. Gallo stepped down the slope a little from the unit and kept a close eye on the beasts in the canal as the other three scanned the ground.

Carefully, not wanting to attract too much attention from the crocs, the other three approached Dog, who was busy tearing into something. So intent was the mutt on his meal that Scriptor had to push him away to look at what it was he was eating. It was clearly meat of some kind, but it had mostly already been consumed by the crocodiles, and Dog had been tearing at the fragments that were left. The meat had stained the dirt pink, and that colour confirmed their suspicions. Those other pink stains had all been where meat had lain on the ground until the crocs had eaten it.

Callie frowned at the sight and shivered. Not a good thing to have found, given what the discovery suggested. Gingerly, Uncle Scriptor picked up the straggly meat and threw it down into the canal, where it disappeared with a splash, and four big scaly beasts immediately turned and sploshed in after it, startling Gallo who was now watching nearby.

Gently patting Dog and then encouraging him back up the slope towards the Romans, Marcus started walking, letting his gaze wander back and forth across the slope as he ascended, trying to spot anything else of interest.

As the dog ran over to Potens for a stroke, Uncle Scriptor paused and then took a detour, walking in a wide arc back towards them, close to the labyrinth plateau that loomed above the slope. Frowning, Marcus and Callie followed him. As he reached his goal, the standard bearer stopped and scratched his chin, trying to make sense of what he was seeing. Marcus and Callie peered intently at the sight. First the tracks of crocodiles and of the dog, interspersed with the marks where chunks of meat had lain on the ground and now, here, they had found an area of sand and dust that had been disturbed quite thoroughly and quite recently. It could have been a man, possibly dragging something heavy, from the marks, but it was hard to tell. One thing for certain was that they were not made by crocodiles or dogs.

'What do you make of that?'

Marcus and Callie shared a blank look and the girl shrugged as Marcus pictured Egyptian gods rising from the sand. He shook his head at his own imagination. 'Of course,' their uncle sighed. 'There was a lookout who ran back and warned the men. This was probably where he had been sitting.' A moment later Gallo joined them and they wandered up the slope again until they came to where the others had gathered in a small knot, discussing the situation. Brutus fell silent and waited expectantly as the four of them approached.

'What did you find?' Potens asked quietly.

'Interesting things, if a little worrying,' Uncle Scriptor replied. 'Someone left a trail of meat up the slope from the canal. The crocs didn't purposefully come up here to attack you – they were just following a trail of food. Someone led them up here.'

'Who would do that, sir?' Brutus asked in confusion.

'And where did they get meat?' added Senex.

'Good questions both,' Gallo replied. 'I looked at the mess as I came up the slope. There wasn't enough left of the meat to tell what it was, so we won't know where it came from. As to who did it? Well, I don't know that either, but we've apparently been cursed by the crocodile god, and we saw something down in the labyrinth that looked an awful lot like the big croc-headed one himself.'

Brutus frowned and opened his mouth to speak.

'Don't ask,' interrupted Gallo. 'We'll tell you all about it when we're back in camp with the others and settling down for the evening. I think we need to go and get some shut-eye now. In the safety of the camp. But the fact remains that someone or something definitely doesn't like us being here. I'm beginning to think that miserable old seer was right.'

Marcus frowned as a thought struck him. 'Where *is* the seer?'

'To be honest,' Maximus said, looking a little sheepish, 'we've been leaving him to his own devices. He's not good company. All he does is complain and grumble. Last we saw of him he was up the slope near the ruins. Then we forgot all about him in the excitement of the attack. If he has any sense he ran miles away when the crocs came.'

'I hope not,' Gallo grumbled. 'We have a scroll I want him to translate for us.'

Turning, he peered around in the evening gloom. The light was almost gone now, and it was hard to make out much detail.

'Seer?' the centurion yelled. There was no reply, and the others began to shout 'Seer' and wander around the area at the top of the slope. Marcus tapped his lip as he watched. Finally, he smiled and crouched down.

'Dog?'

The unit's new mascot ran over to him, wagging, and he ruffled the hair on the dog's head.

'Dog? Find the seer. The old man. Seer?' Marcus asked, doing a passable impression of the old man's grumbling voice and then standing slightly stooped and glowering just as the old man was known to do.

Dog seemed to get the idea, snuffled around the floor and scuttled off, wagging as he searched. Marcus grinned and followed him, Callie and their uncle close behind. The three of them pursued the dog across the slope until he stopped by a low ruined wall at the labyrinth's edge. There, a deep pile of sand had drifted up in the lee of the stone, and Dog started digging, wagging animatedly.

Marcus cleared his throat as he spotted a piece of threadbare brown wool in the shadow at the bottom of the wall. Wool beneath the pile of sand...

'Seer?'

The heap shuddered for a moment and then fell away as the seer revealed himself. The sand had not in fact been a deep pile, but a shallow sprinkling over the top of the old man who had pulled a cloak over himself and hidden there, using cupped hands to shower loose sand over the top of himself.

'An explanation would be good about now?' Uncle Scriptor said, quietly but forcefully.

The old man gave him an unhappy look. 'Why couldn't you just leave me alone? First you open a sacred place and bring a curse down on us all, and then you go off exploring and leave me with just those legionary thugs who I wouldn't trust as far as I could throw one of them, and then an army of crocodiles attack! I was well hidden, and the sand would have covered my scent. No crocodile would have found me. But now here I am again, and now I'm in danger all over again.'

The standard bearer shook his head. 'Has anyone ever told you that you complain too much? And anyway, you weren't well enough hidden from crocs, or Dog wouldn't have been able to find you.'

'I wish you would let me go.'

'Well we won't. Not until we're done here. Once the centurion has a cart of gold and we're heading north you can go where you like, and I'll even give you a bonus. But for now, we still need you. In the labyrinth we found a small library and we've brought a scroll up which we would like you to read.'

Straightening, the seer shook himself down, scattering sand and rock about, and then followed as the others trudged back across to the centurion who stood with Potens and Senex.

Wordlessly, Gallo handed over the papyrus and the old seer took it with narrowed eyes and unravelled it, scanning down it quickly.

'It's too dark to read it properly now. Can it wait?'

Gallo nodded. 'Read it through in the morning.'

'Were there any others like this one?'

'No. Scriptor seemed to think it was misplaced.'

'It's very old.'

'I know,' the centurion replied. 'Come on. Let's get into the safety of the camp. We'll start again in the morning.'

CHAPTER 10

Callie's journal

Yesterday was one of the most frightening days of my life, and one of the most exciting. And despite the monster we met in the tunnels and the crocodile attack on the camp, we are close now – so close we can almost feel it.

Marcus and I saved the day, I think. This morning, the seer examined the scroll I brought back. It was clearly an amazing find – the thing we really needed. Marcus was lucky to find the missing section that identified the scroll as important and overlooked. But best of all is that I have learned enough of the language in the past week to correct the old seer when he misread parts.

Not only did the scroll contain the simple map which showed the pyramid and the labyrinth, as well as the canal nearby, but the text had been a worker or architect's account of the pyramid's construction, even detailing a number of surprises the tomb held for the unwary. Without its warnings, we might have been in real trouble when we got inside.

I think we have proved ourselves enough now that Centurion Gallo will not leave us behind again. Now I cannot wait to see what is inside the pyramid.

'Do you think the map was right?' Gallo fretted. 'I mean, it was hardly an engineering diagram done by a sensible, educated Roman professional, but more a drawing done by some loincloth-clad ancient Egyptian with a fake beard and a weird obsession with crocodiles. It might be a long way from accurate.'

Callie shrugged. 'There's every chance it's completely wrong, sir. But it is the only lead we have to go on, and don't forget what the old seer read.'

Marcus nodded, thinking back on the morning when the seer had scanned down the parchment scroll with the aid of Callie and their uncle, his sister's small knowledge of Egyptian helping put the daft, doddering old man straight when he wandered off-subject.

'We'll know soon enough, anyway,' their uncle added, nodding towards the work party. Marcus watched them tensely.

As soon as breakfast had been finished and the men had packed everything up, the unit had come round to the south side of the pyramid, between it and the labyrinth platform. Potens had taken charge as soon as they had arrived, detailing the men into work parties and drawing lines in the dirt with a big stick, Callie helping him where she could and when she was permitted.

While Secundus had taken charge of the defences, setting men on watch in all directions – especially towards the canal – and a small group to guard the hole which led down into the labyrinth, Potens had begun to excavate.

He had announced that if what they thought of as the underground labyrinth had actually originally been *above* ground, and just the lower of two floors, then it could be fifteen or even twenty feet down to the original ground level. Having marked out an area on the ground relating to the position of the entrance on the map, Potens had set to work.

Two tent-parties of eight men dug the soft, giving ground with their shovels and threw it up into the open space. Another party of eight at each side took away the spoil heaps as much as they could to prevent it building up and then just collapsing into the hole again, as it does when building a fort in sand on a beach. A final party of eight worked with the engineer himself, clearing off the stonework of the pyramid as it was revealed by the digging, and examining it for marks or cracks.

Gallo had sent a further group of eight off to find a local farm and acquire a cart and oxen from them. When they found the treasure of pharaoh Amenemhat the Third, they would need some way to transport it back to Alexandria. The men sent out would bring back just such a cart, whether its owner was happy to get rid of it or not but, unlike many army officers, Gallo knew how important it was to try and stay on good terms with the natives, so the soldiers had taken a pouch of coins with them, and the poor farmer would be handsomely paid for his troubles.

All was now prepared and Marcus and Callie could do nothing but wait and watch the pyramid being gradually revealed. Despite having been told about the rising ground level several times – engineers always seemed to think you wanted telling the details over and over again, even when you yawned wide – it had surprised Marcus to see just how much of the pyramid's heavy sloping stone side was buried beneath the sand, and watching it being uncovered was strangely exciting.

His eyes strayed upwards into the bright hot morning light and to the point at the top of the pyramid, the white face of the structure almost blinding in the sun.

'That's a lot of limestone,' he murmured, picturing that enormous amount of heavy stone above him and shivering despite the heat. He had an unfortunate fear of heights rather than confined spaces like he'd heard some people had, though he could easily imagine picking up that terror too in the next few hours.

Uncle Scriptor, standing close by, nodded. 'Imagine how many forts, palaces and villas we could build with the stone from just one pyramid.'

Potens, busy working hard, paused at the comment and turned. 'Actually, only the outer face is limestone; and probably the very middle, where the tomb is. Most of the pyramids are made from darker, less decorative stone, or more

174

often from baked mud bricks. This white is just a coating on the outside to make it smooth and impressive.'

'It works,' Marcus muttered.

'Hey! I think I've got something,' one of the legionaries shouted and Potens dropped down into the lowest level of the work pit and rushed over to where the legionaries were digging. Among them Maximus, his muscles moving beneath his skin like cats in a bag, shovelled some more of the sand out of the way so that the engineer could get a better look.

Marcus narrowed his eyes to a squint, partially due to the brightness of the morning, which was already beginning to feel unbearably hot – and he wasn't even doing any work! – and partially to try and see what was happening among the small group of men working by the flat stone surface in the pit. As a long discussion among the gathered workers continued with no sign of an end coming, the centurion cleared his throat meaningfully and began to tap his foot. Potens stepped to one side and pointed and Marcus shuffled round the pit's lip towards Gallo to see what he could see.

At the pit's lowest surface, there was a different colour of stone. The white stopped, and a brown colour began, still mostly buried. Gallo smiled broadly and Marcus felt a grin burst out on his own face. They had found the entrance exactly where they had expected from reading the scroll and its rough map. It was hard to believe their luck! A sigh of relief hissed from the centurion as the watchers realised they would indeed be taking a cart load of gold home to the prefect, and probably today.

'Excellent. The entrance,' Gallo smiled, and Marcus wondered why Potens' own expression was less than pleased. 'What's the matter, sir?' he asked.

'Pyramids are covered with white limestone, led.'

'Yes, we know that,' the centurion snapped.

'And the entrance we've just located is of brown mud-brick.'

'Well yes!'

Understanding dawned on Marcus and he felt the grin slide from his face. 'But pyramid entrances were hidden, sir,' he interjected.

'Yes.' Gallo was starting to sound irritated now.

'Beneath the white limestone outer,' Potens added helpfully.

'So...' it suddenly struck the centurion, and Marcus watched the unpleasant realisation dawn like a cloud crossing the sun, 'this entrance should be covered up by the white stone.'

'Yes sir.'

'And it isn't.'

'No sir.'

'So this entrance is not hidden?'

'No sir. Just buried in sand. Not hidden.'

'So what you're telling me is that we are not the first people to set eyes upon this entrance?'

'No sir.'

Marcus' heart sank. After all they had gone through it appeared that this pyramid had already been robbed just like so many others – *most* of the others in Egypt, in fact. The very idea that they might have to return to Alexandria and face the prefect empty handed was nerve-wracking, even for Marcus. He couldn't imagine how the centurion was feeling. Turbo would be extremely angry. There would be repercussions… possibly demotions and punishment. He felt the chances of him joining the unit when he came of age, let alone early, sliding away with the last vestiges of his smile.

And even if the prefect accepted their failure calmly, they might have to go back to the library, do some more research, choose another possible pyramid and then travel over half of Egypt and start again from scratch.

'Bum!' announced Gallo with feeling.

Potens nodded, clearly sharing his commander's appraisal of the situation. The centurion, his expression churning with anger and irritation, turned and spotted the old seer sitting in the shade of a broken wall. 'You!'

'Me?' asked the old man, rising, creaking, to his feet.

'Yes, you. Will the pyramid have been robbed if the door has already been opened?'

The old seer shrugged. 'I'm no expert, but I would think so. Wouldn't you?'

Gallo stamped across angrily to the excavation. 'Well I'm not going all the way back to Alexandria without at least having a look. Get that sand cleared out of the way and we'll go in and look around. Even if it *was* robbed before, perhaps they couldn't carry everything and left some valuables for us.'

The engineer nodded and began to direct his men again, the legionaries bending with renewed effort to shovel everything out of the way. Gradually as Marcus watched the open dark doorway was revealed and sun shone into the inside of the pyramid for the first time since... well, since who knew when?

When Potens and his workers had finished and cleared away enough space for a man to fit through, Senex used his flint and iron and started a small flame, from which half a dozen men lit torches.

'I'm going in,' Gallo announced. 'And Senex, Scriptor, and Potens.' He caught a look on Uncle Scriptor's face and nodded. 'The children too. Whatever's in the pyramid is probably less dangerous than swanning about near a canal full of crocs while you wait. Dog stays up here, though. In addition, I want Maximus and Brutus to bring the seer in with us.'

'In there?' the old native paled and started to shake his head.

'Don't panic. It looks like the place is empty now anyway so you'll have nothing to worry about.' Leaving the old seer to be escorted inside by the two enormous legionaries, Gallo took one of the burning torches from Potens as he passed them around, and then the group gathered together, the engineer at the front, Marcus and Callie lining up behind their uncle.

Peering into the dark aperture, Potens looked over his shoulder. 'It slopes down straight away, so watch your step as we enter. As soon as we're in we'll pause before we descend any further.'

'Alright. Let's go inside and have a look,' Gallo said with a resigned sigh.

At the centurion's command the party of nine moved into the pyramid entrance and paused just inside, staggered down the sloping tunnel with its shallow steps, to let their eyes adjust to the darkness after the brilliant sunshine of the Egyptian morning.

'Looks like whoever was in here before us was here pretty recently,' the centurion noted, pointing at the floor. The others looked down. The dust and sand of the floor was showing signs of being disturbed.

'Possibly, sir,' Uncle Scriptor agreed. 'But we can't be too sure. No air could get in here, so after the stones initially settled there would be no new dust falling and no breeze to disturb what was here. Any marks on the floor could be a thousand years old, but still fresh as yesterday's.'

Marcus sagged again, what felt like the last ray of hope whisked away from him by the logic of his uncle's words.

'Alright. On we go,' called Potens from the front. 'Scriptor, you and Callie need to warn me of anything you read about in the scroll.'

On down the slope the Romans went for what felt like ages, deep into the pyramid. The corridor was long and dark, and only just wide enough for a man to move through comfortably, but higher than two tall men. It was an oddly-grand entrance, and a little bit creepy.

'When we get to the bottom,' Callie said from the middle of the group, 'there's a room with another corridor leading off. If the scroll was correct, there was a huge stone block that would have been dropped across the room to block it when the pyramid was sealed. If the block is in place, then no one can have been any further inside. If they have, they must have somehow got through the block.'

Slowly, the group reached the bottom of the stairs and moved out into a spacious, dark chamber that felt eerily cold after the warm outside. Marcus shivered as the torches picked out the paintings and endless hieroglyphic writings all over the walls, though his sister moved across to them and began to examine them intently. While she might have a fascination for the odd language – and gods knew she was picking it up fast – he was more intent now on finding the heart of the pyramid and probably extinguishing that last spark of hope that they might achieve their goal. Much could ride on this mission. Not for Callie. Clearly for Gallo and his men. But also for Marcus. A successful mission, especially one in which he'd played an active part, could seriously increase his chances of being signed up for the legion early.

'I'll never get to take the oath,' he muttered under his breath, quietly adding his whisper to the general susurration of the legionaries discussing their surroundings and of Callie sounding out passages from the wall paintings.

'What oath?' Uncle Scriptor asked quietly from behind him, making him jump. He turned, his heart racing. He hadn't realised the big man was there.

'The military oath,' he said quietly and despondently. 'If this place is empty and the unit fails prefect Turbo your

181

reputations will suffer and any chance I have of joining up early will vanish.'

His uncle dropped to a crouch facing him. 'Why do you need to join us early, Marcus? Why do you need to join us at all?' Marcus frowned in confusion, and his uncle sighed. 'It all looks adventurous, but it's a very dangerous career. Remember your father. He was pensioned out after he lost the use of his arm. Luckily he'd made centurion and he'd put plenty of money away, so he could afford to set up his business. Most soldiers who that happens to become beggars. You know I've been putting money away for you and Callie – I've no kids of my own, obviously, and I can't see myself having them. I'll look after you. When you're old enough I can set you up in business like your dad. You don't need to join the army.'

Marcus shook his head. 'But I do, Uncle. Callie might be happy frittering away her life on learning and hobbies, but since dad… Since you started looking after us, the army is my life now. It fed me and clothed me and put a roof over my head when we needed help. What else should I do? Besides, even trading can be dangerous. Ships can be lost in the Cretan Sea,' he reminded his uncle, who looked sad and contrite at the memory.

'Whether we succeed or fail on this mission, the prefect is not the only one who can bend the rules for you, Marcus. With the permission of the tribunes or the camp prefect, Centurion Gallo could push through the application. But you need to be a bit older yet.' His uncle gave him an appraising look and smiled. 'What say we begin sword and shield practice when we get back to Alexandria? Give you a head start. That might help the centurion's application for you.'

Marcus broke into a grateful smile. Despite their dismal progress with the mission, it seemed that he might still have a chance.

'Where's this block, then?' Gallo asked, his voice echoing round the chamber and drawing their attention.

Callie turned from the wall she was examining, tapping her pen on her wax table and peering around. 'They got rid of it? How? That's *impossible!*'

'I'd have to agree with Callie,' Potens said to the centurion. 'I've seen these blocks used in other pyramids in the north. It's probably twenty tons of rock. Not easy to shift and would take weeks to break through. There would be evidence in the middle of the room, and the floor's empty.'

The soldiers spread out, examining the room, and Marcus, left in the middle, found himself frowning and slowly tilting his head back to look up. His heart froze and his bladder threatened to leak again as he realised that the huge twenty ton block of stone was suspended right over his head, visible as a slightly different colour to the rest of the ceiling. In a panic, he leapt up and stepped out from underneath it.

'Erm, Sir?'

Gallo turned from where he was peering into a dark corner. 'Yes?'

'Look up, sir!'

Potens, Gallo and Scriptor arrived together at his side, peering up into the darkness and showing far more interest and a lot less fear than Marcus thought sensible.

'It's not come down! How is that possible?' Uncle Scriptor frowned.

'I have no idea,' the engineer admitted. 'They always build these things the same way. The room's filled with sand and the block plonked on top. Then, when they seal the place up, they just remove the sand and the huge block falls into place and seals it tight. So how has it stayed up?'

'I don't care,' Gallo said, 'but I don't recommend standing underneath it, in case it suddenly decides it's had enough of hovering in the air and drops on you. We'd be able to carry you back rolled up, you'd be so flat!'

'There *will be* a scientific explanation,' Potens said, peering up into the darkness. 'I just don't know what it is. If we're here for another day or two I'd love to look closely into it.'

'That, Potens, is because all you engineers are mad. Come on. Where next?'

Potens pointed to a passageway ahead, partially filled with rubble. 'That looks favourite,' he said.

'That's a trick,' Callie said, running her finger down the writing on the wall. 'It's designed to misdirect us and slow us down. In fact, I think there might be a trap that way. Look.' Moving her pointing finger from one line of pictures to another, she grinned and stepped into the wall, disappearing. Confused, the rest of them crossed the chamber to where the girl had been, Marcus quickly jumping across underneath the hovering block and hurrying along to catch up.

Arriving ahead of the adults, he peered at the wall where his sister had disappeared. Another tunnel led from this room – a much smaller affair than the rubble-strewn one. It had been enclosed and concealed by wooden doors painted the same as the chamber's walls. If Callie had not known they were there and opened them, there was every chance the Romans would never have found the second tunnel. He peeked between the doors to see Callie lurking inside. 'This way,' she grinned at him.

Chilled by the ancient cold air down here, the small party moved into the new corridor in single file, Scriptor stepping out ahead this time with Callie and Marcus close behind, the

185

centurion following on. The long, narrow corridor was not painted or covered in writing, and felt very eerie to the Romans following it. Finally, after what seemed an age, they saw the corridor turn left and, as they followed it around the bend, Scriptor paused and gestured to the others, holding up his torch.

'Same again. Odd, isn't it?'

The others looked up at the block seemingly hovering at ceiling level, which should by rights be blocking the way ahead. With a slow step to peer up at the impossible trap, Uncle Scriptor led them on down the next corridor, Marcus hurrying past the suspended block. A few long moments later the party of Roman adventurers were directed to look up once again by Scriptor.

'That's the third of three. And all three blocks have apparently never been lowered. Or they were somehow raised again, of course. I expect that, given the time and opportunity, Potens and I could work out how it was done and why. But it doesn't clear anything up at the moment. It doesn't answer what happened here.'

'How far to the treasure?' Gallo asked.

'Just round the corner,' smiled Uncle Scriptor and stepped away, disappearing into the next passage. Marcus and Callie followed him and the short corridor led into a chamber, just large enough for the nine of them to stand in. The walls were once more covered with paintings and hieroglyphics, but the floor was bare and the room was empty.

'Is this it?' Gallo sagged.

Callie nodded. 'This is the ante-chamber where the treasure would be kept.' She pointed at an opening. 'Through there is the burial chamber itself. There would probably be more in there, as well as the mummy of the pharaoh and the jars with his parts in them.'

Old Senex sniffed. 'You can bet that if this room is empty, then so is that one. In there would be his golden coffin, and no treasure hunter would pass that one up.'

'So this has all been one great big waste of time,' sighed Marcus as the centurion wandered across and leaned through the door with his arm extended so that his torch lit the burial chamber beyond. Marcus peered into the opening – it too was empty, apart from a large, heavy stone sarcophagus which lay open. Though there were things in the room nothing glinted in the light, and Marcus stayed with the others, letting the centurion go and check the room thoroughly. He did not feel like poking around a dead pharaoh when there was clearly no gold there to satisfy the prefect and make it worthwhile.

'The place has been thoroughly looted,' Gallo confirmed, re-emerging. 'We'll have to start all over again.'

Uncle Scriptor leaned against the wall and scratched his chin.

'You might be right, sir, but I would ask that we stay another night. Give Potens, Senex and I a chance to try and piece together what happened here. Simple robbery doesn't explain how the huge stone blocks that are supposed to seal it shut are open. And then there's the missing scrolls from the labyrinth library. Not to mention the statue that attacked us down there and the mysterious trail of meat that led the crocs to the men. There is a lot more to this than meets the eye.'

Gallo nodded and Marcus sighed. While he felt completely let down, and despite the failure of the mission and the fact that they all baulked at the thought of having to do all this again somewhere else, there were questions he too would like to know the answers to.

'Alright,' Gallo harrumphed.

'That's a waste of time,' the old native seer grumbled, looking nervously at the door. They turned in surprise to face him. It was the first time the old fool had spoken since they entered the pyramid and his presence had been all but forgotten. 'This place is empty,' the seer grumbled. 'It's been looted already. We might as well go. And I can be of no use to you now, not that I've been any help before. Let me go north again, and I suggest you do too.'

Gallo waved a finger at him.

'One more night will cost us nothing, old man. And if my clever lads can work something out we'll at least be able to explain to the prefect *why* we returned empty handed.' He turned to Uncle Scriptor, who was still clearly deep in thought. 'We will go outside and tell the men what's happening. You and Potens can stay here if you like, and explore some more?'

The two men looked at each other, and Scriptor shook his head. 'I think we need to come out first, sir. We'll bring a few lamps down here and a load more torches, and a ladder for the climb. We'll get all the tools we need and then do a proper job of examining the place.'

Gallo shrugged and the whole group turned, defeated, to leave the empty, looted pyramid.

CHAPTER 11

The party of nine emerged once more into the searing golden sun of the Egyptian morning, blinding and headache-inducing after the cool darkness of the pyramid. Senex was the first out and he paused, waiting for the two huge legionaries and the native seer they escorted, and then wandered off with them towards the small campfire where a dozen or more soldiers were busy cooking an early lunch.

Potens and Gallo followed, with Marcus and Callie and their uncle stepping out last, stretching and turning their faces up to the sun with their eyes closed, relishing the warmth after the chill inside the pyramid. Movement flickered in the corner of Marcus' eye but he ignored it, drinking in the sun's rays.

As they stood for a long moment, Marcus tried not to chew over the results of their mission, but he failed as he had every other time on the journey back out. *Nothing*! Not a single gold coin. Not even an interesting *bean*. Gallo was extremely irritated, as Marcus could see from his face. The centurion would end up being short-tempered with the men whether he intended to or not, and Marcus realised that he and Callie would have to stay out of Gallo's way and lie low for a while. Somehow, Marcus had never really believed they would fail in their task. The 22nd legion were the heroes of the east, and in the three years Marcus and his sister had lodged with them, Gallo's century had always succeeded in everything they did.

Marcus was proud of his uncle's century, and it nagged at him that even with the best men in the army they had still failed.

But then, could *anyone* have succeeded? Gallo was the bravest man he had ever met. Potens could build or take apart anything, given the time. Senex knew the will of the gods and could interpret omens. Scriptor was simply clever. And Maximus and Brutus could lift the world from its hinges if they had to. If *this lot* could not succeed then *no one* could.

Marcus opened his eyes and his gaze strayed across the platform that formed the roof of the labyrinth, covered in its pieces of wall and column, until he realised that the movement that had flickered in the corner of his eye was that of carts and men actively busying themselves among the ruins.

Confused, he squinted into the bright sunlight. Gallo's over-zealous men had apparently acquired *three* carts rather than the one he had ordered, and the vehicles were standing among the ruins with the oxen that pulled them snorting and bored. A dozen or more of the legionaries left outside had stopped excavating now that the entrance was clear and were instead loading something into the carts.

'What are they doing?' he asked, frowning.

Scriptor, Gallo and Potens joined him and peered off across the flat ground. The latter smiled. 'Gathering the old marble, lad. I told them when we sent the parties out this morning that if they had spare cart space they should gather up any bits of broken marble from around the ruins to take with us.'

'Broken marble,' questioned Marcus curiously. 'Why?'

Potens shrugged. 'It's doing no good here among the ruins, but we can take it back with us since we have the carts anyway. You see…' he acquired that strange, happy, far-away look that engineers always got when they had the chance to explain something dull and complicated to non-engineers. 'Marble can be rendered down to make lime, and lime is an essential part of concrete. In fact 'marble lime' is one of the best types of lime for making concrete. And the prefect will need a lot of concrete to rebuild Alexandria. So I thought we'd fill up any space around the treasure with marble pieces just to help. And since there's no treasure, we might as well at least take the marble, as it'll help anyway.'

Marcus nodded, his attention only half on the explanation.

'You see, what happens, is that…'

'Ha!' yelled Callie suddenly, and smacked her forehead with the palm of her hand as she stared in amazement at the carts being loaded.

The soldiers frowned as Marcus turned towards Callie.

'What is it, sis?'

'The carts,' she grinned. 'The old man. I've got it!'

'Got what?' Potens asked.

'And whatever it is, don't give me it,' grumbled Gallo.

But Callie was smiling so wide it looked like the top half of her head might fall off. 'Come with me.'

Marcus could do little other than scurry along in his sister's wake as she marched off to where the soldiers were making their food. Among them, the old native seer crouched, grinding up salted meat and vegetables in a bronze bowl to make soup.

'You!' Callie pointed at the seer and the old man turned in surprise.

'What, girl?'

'Where is the treasure going?' Callie demanded. Marcus blinked in surprise.

'What?' repeated the old man.

'Where is the treasure going? Has it been loaded on ships yet, or is it still stored?'

The old man's eyes flicked nervously from side to side, but he blustered at her as the soldiers gathered around him. 'I have no idea what you're talking about.'

Uncle Scriptor narrowed his eyes at Callie, and then grinned and gestured at Maximus and Brutus nearby. 'Hold him.'

The two big legionaries stepped across past the fire and grabbed hold of the old man's shoulders, holding him tight.

The seer struggled for a moment, but he was clearly no match for the strength of the two brutes.

'I think you *do* know what she's talking about, don't you, *Inkaef*!'

Centurion Gallo shook his head in confusion. 'Who in the name of all the gods is *Inkaef*?'

'*He* is,' replied Scriptor smugly, and the seer started to look panicked. 'Inkaef is the high priest of Sobek in Crocodilopolis. He's the man we went to see but they said wasn't there because he was away on cult business!'

Marcus grinned with realisation as the centurion turned his puzzled gazes on the seer, who had stopped struggling and was standing straight now, proudly. Marcus laughed, his gaze darting back and forth between his grinning sister and the old man.

'Look!' Callie said as she stepped forward, stretched as high as she could and hooked the old man's necklace out of his clothing, showing the smooth, triangular pendant. 'It's a crocodile tooth. We should have seen that from the start. And the crocodile mummification priest at the great temple in the city was wearing one too. He was fiddling nervously with it. I bet that if we looked, every Sobek priest has one!'

Marcus stared at the tooth. How had he missed such an obvious connection? 'I'll bet that's why none of the cult have been willing to help us wherever we've gone,' he said suddenly. 'The old man's always been lurking around behind us while we talked. We thought it was because he was frightened and wanted to leave, but it was really so that he could wave at his priests from behind us – tell them to pretend not to know him and to give us no help.'

He thought back over their meeting with the priest in Crocodilopolis. It certainly fitted.

'So when he got bitten by that croc back in Terenouthis…?' the centurion's jaw hardened.

Callie nodded. 'He wasn't really in trouble at all. He did get nibbled, but that was because he'd picked up a baby croc and then hid it under his robe with his bad arm. Then that night he snuck into the tent and put it next to me. It might already have been dead before Uncle squashed it – I don't know – but I think he hoped it would frighten us into turning back.'

Gallo frowned. 'But why did he *want* us to turn back, anyway? I mean it's not as if we've stolen his pharaoh's treasure!'

Callie grinned. 'True. But he wanted us to go home so that we didn't find out that it was *him* who stole the treasure, isn't that right, high priest Inkaef?'

The old seer simply sneered at them.

'Him?' said Gallo and Potens together in surprise.

'Yes, him,' the standard bearer smiled victoriously, placing his hands on his nephew and niece's shoulders proudly. 'Sacred or not, native cults don't get the financial support they used to before Rome ruled here. I think probably a lot of their priests have taken to a little robbery to help pay the bills. Inkaef here and a few of his fellow croc-cultists stole all Amenemhat's treasure not long ago. The amazing and irritating thing is that we've stood a few paces away from it, haven't we, Cal?'

The old man began to struggle in his captors' grasp again, but the two giant legionaries held him tight.

'That's what made me think of it,' Callie said, pointing at the workers on the plateau. 'They're loading carts that were meant for the treasure. And I suddenly remembered when we were at the library in Alexandria. As we went in, there were carts unloading into a warehouse opposite. And as we left the place again, we mentioned the pyramid by name. The high priest was there in disguise as a peasant, watching the treasure leaving the carts and going into storage. He tried to stop us coming here but he failed, and you dragged him along with us instead. I bet you really ruined his day!'

Marcus grinned. 'The treasure is supposed to stay in the warehouse until he's sold it on, I expect.'

The centurion wagged a finger at the old man. 'So *he* was also the one who left the trail of meat up from the canal and enticed the crocs into attacking the lads.'

Uncle Scriptor nodded. 'He had plenty of opportunity. No one watched him, you see. No one ever does, because he's so harmless and he complains all the time, so he was free to raid the supplies and leave the trail. And while he was there, he rolled in the mud to darken his body, and then slipped down into the labyrinth. I'm assuming he had a crocodile mask down there already, possibly for some cult ritual, but he put it on to scare us in the tunnels.'

'It worked too!' agreed Gallo, wide-eyed.

'And then when we came out, he followed us, leaving his mask in there somewhere. While we were fighting off the crocs with the fire, he buried himself in sand to hide the fact that he was already covered in the stuff!'

Gallo shook his head. 'But how could he navigate around the labyrinth?'

Callie took up the story again. 'I expect he and his priest friends have been going in there for years. They must have some other easier entrance somewhere. It was them who took all the missing scrolls from the library room. They took everything that helped them find the entrance to the pyramid. Then they went in and looted it. That's why the entrance was already open and the blocks inside had somehow been wedged back up. We were very lucky someone long ago had misfiled one of the important scrolls, or they would have taken that too and we would never have got in.'

The centurion nodded. 'All very neat. And that means the treasure we're after is already in Alexandria, right under the prefect's nose!'

'Probably,' corrected Marcus. Alexandria was a port, with shipping links all over the empire. By now the treasure could be bobbing across the waves bound for another province.

A commotion suddenly broke out as the old seer stamped down hard on Brutus' foot. The big man gasped in surprise and for just a moment his grip loosened. Maximus, taken off guard, felt the seer's arm slip out of his own grasp, and the old man was running.

Scriptor and Gallo shouted and legionaries drew their swords as the thieving high priest scrambled away up the slope surprisingly fast. If he could get out of sight, he would almost certainly escape, since he was a local and knew every hiding place while the rest of them were all strangers here. As the century of men began to give chase, a familiar shape appeared at the crest of the hill ahead of the running thief.

Dog pulled back his lips, baring his sharp teeth, and growled menacingly at the priest, who stumbled to a halt in fear of the animal that blocked his path. Before he could do anything else, Maximus and Brutus had caught up with him again and gripped him tight. With little effort they lifted him off the ground between them so that he couldn't stamp down again. As they returned him to the centurion and the campfire area, the old man spat at them.

'You're too late anyway!'

Uncle Scriptor grabbed his robe at the neck and twisted it, pulling the old man close.

'Where is the treasure now?'

'It's still in the warehouse, Roman. But it's been sold to a private collector on Crete for more money than you could possibly imagine. The ship from Crete arrives on the first of the month and will load the treasure and sail straight away. You don't have time to stop it!'

Gallo and Scriptor exchanged a look of defeat and Marcus felt his spirits sink. The new month was only three days away, and it had taken them five days of fast marching to get here. 'Even if we go as fast as we can, I really don't think we can make it in time,' Uncle Scriptor sighed, and the old thief laughed triumphantly.

'We might if we take a boat,' Marcus narrowed his eyes.

'A boat? But that takes *longer*,' Gallo frowned.

'It takes longer going *up*stream, sir! *Down*stream will be fast,' Marcus grinned. 'And we can take a swift boat that only carries a few men. They had them back at the Nile, and on the canal.'

A smile slid across the centurion's face. 'Most of the lads can march back and meet us there later. Secundus can lead them, while the eight of us take this thief back, claim the treasure and deliver him to the authorities for trial.'

'Three days,' Scriptor smiled as he hugged the children proudly. 'We *can* do it.'

CHAPTER 12

Centurion Gallo of the 22nd Deiotaran legion had been leaning back against the warm stone of the Serapeum temple, allowing the sun to bathe him, but at the sound of a horn blast he pulled himself upright.

Halfway down the steps Scriptor stood, once more in full kit with his sweaty leopard pelt draped over his helmet and the glinting standard of the century pointing up into the blue cloudless sky, Marcus and Callie at his sides. Old Senex stood near them, along with Potens, both men smiling in the sunshine.

On the lowest step the man they had come to think of as the old seer, but who was in truth Inkaef – high priest of the Crocodile God – sat dejectedly, his ankles and wrists tied tightly with rope. Enormous Maximus with his overhanging brow and huge Brutus with his bull tattoos loomed on either side of the prisoner and Dog stood in front of him, giving a deep, angry growl every time the man so much as twitched.

The horn sounded again, much closer, and the six soldiers straightened as if on parade. Marcus emulated them, straight as a board, while Callie lounged, practicing her hieroglyphics on her wax tablet – she believed she had worked out her name in Egyptian, now. On the far side of the city's ruinous walls the air was filled with the sounds of chiselling and hammering as legionary masons shaped blocks of stone to repair the city while others erected wooden scaffolding around ruined buildings.

The third horn blast made their ears ring and a moment later prefect Turbo rounded the corner astride a pure white horse, his red cloak settled behind him and his decorative helmet glittering in the sun. The standards of his personal guard came close behind, and two dozen dangerous looking men all on horseback, each armed with a spear and wearing a white uniform.

'Centurion Gallo?'

'Yes, my lord,' the centurion smiled, saluting.

'Your messenger said I should come quickly. I am not accustomed to being summoned by the people who work for me… that is not how things are done. I was not even aware you were back in the city. Perhaps you should have thought to visit my headquarters first and announced your return, rather than sending for me as though I were a servant?'

The prefect's eyes flashed dangerously. He was irritated, and rumour had it that very bad things happened when Turbo became irritated.

'My apologies, sir,' Gallo replied, stepping down the three stairs to stand before the prefect. 'It was a matter of timing. We had to prevent a great haul leaving Egypt before we could impound it.'

The prefect raised an eyebrow.

'If you would accompany me, sir?'

Turbo frowned, but dropped down from his horse, dusting his hands together and passing the reins to one of his men. 'Most of your century seems to be absent, Centurion.'

'They are still returning by foot, sir. We few came by boat in order to catch the treasure of pharaoh Amenemhat the Third leaving for Crete, where a private collector has apparently paid a large amount of money for it. The old man on the steps over there is the high priest of Sobek, and it was he who had stolen the treasure that we went in search of.'

As he finished talking, Gallo stepped into the warehouse. The prefect followed him and came to a halt just inside, clearly visible through the wide double doors from the steps opposite where Marcus and Callie watched with wide grins. The huge room was lit by open panels in the roof – after all, it never rained here. A wide area in the centre of the room had been left clear, but both sides were stacked with crates, many of which had had their lids removed to display their contents. Gold and jewels, ebony and silver all glittered in the sunlight. Priceless statues covered in gold and jewelled vases lay amid the riches.

'There is a king's ransom in here,' the prefect said in a whisper.

'Yes sir. Probably enough to pay for Alexandria to be rebuilt and with some left over. And in recovering it, we – or rather, my standard bearer and his wards, to be precise – managed to uncover the thief, who previously occupied a position of responsibility in Egypt as the high priest of the crocodile god.'

The prefect smiled, and the sight warmed the room even further. Straightening and stretching, Turbo placed an arm across Gallo's shoulders in a friendly manner.

'Well done, Centurion. Bravo, and well done indeed. You have not just accomplished your mission, but surpassed it.'

The two men passed back through the entrance and out into the street, where the prefect turned to face the centurion again. 'I will take control from here, Gallo. My bodyguard will arrange for the shipping of this treasure to my vaults. Again, very well done. You and your men look hot, dusty and tired. I would heartily recommend that you take a day of leave with my blessing. Go to the baths. Clean up and have a swim. Then tomorrow morning you should attend my office promptly at first watch. You are a resourceful man, and I might just have another job for you.'

The centurion saluted and sagged slightly as the prefect climbed back on to his horse.

On the steps, Marcus glanced across at Callie and grinned. *Another job? As exciting as this one?* He looked up as the prefect paused while turning his horse away, to smile at them all.

'You don't get sea-sick, do you?' the prefect asked.

Callie's journal

Marcus' luck seems to be spreading. I had hoped that our success would lead to prefect Turbo's aid in pursuing my own task, but it seems I will not have to even ask. Tomorrow the centurion will attend the prefect's office and we will be off on another adventure – a sea one. And given where the treasure was bound, there can only be one destination he has in mind.

Another Roman province's capital. A major hub of trade. The place I have been desperate to visit for three years now.

Crete, here we come.

THE END

(though Marcus and Callie and the men of the 22nd Legion will return soon in 'Pirate Legion')

SCRIPTOR'S FUN FACTS

A **centurion** commanded the main unit of the Roman army – a century. Despite the name, a centurion did not command 100 men, but actually eighty legionaries, split into units of eight men who would share a tent. In addition, a centurion would be aided by an 'optio' – a chosen second in command – a standard bearer, and a musician.

Egypt was one of the most important provinces in the empire. As well as the gold it provided, it also supplied a lot of the grain that was shipped to Rome to make bread. It was so important, in fact, that while other Roman provinces were run by governors from the Roman senate, Egypt was run by a prefect, who was not quite as important as a senator, and therefore could be trusted not to set himself up as sole ruler of Egypt as a senator might.

Pharaoh **Amenemhat III** was so closely involved with the crocodile cult in Egypt that he named his daughter – who ruled Egypt for 4 years herself – Sobekneferu ('Beauty of Sobek'). He abandoned the first pyramid he built and constructed another at Hawara near the Sobek cult's centre of power at the El Fayyum oasis.

Romans relied a great deal on Oracles and **Sacrifices** and the will of the gods. Priests were consulted before any major event and what they said could mean the difference between life and death, war and peace, success and failure. Even in the army, religion was important and rituals and ceremonies were common.

Once upon a time, **crocodiles** were extremely common all the way through Egypt, along the river Nile and in the Oases. In modern times, since the Nile has been dammed in places, there are now no wild crocodiles in Egypt, but in ancient times, they were worshipped as gods, bred in pools and mummified when they died and buried in their own tombs.

The **22nd Deiotariana** – the legion to which Gallo belongs – is the only one of Rome's legions that was not recruited by the emperor. It was left to Rome in a will like a valuable ornament of piece of land. King Deiotarus of Galatia died without children, and he gave his kingdom to Rome entirely. His army stopped being the Royal Galatian army and became the 22nd legion.

Romans wrote on many types of material. Ink was used on papyrus, made from reeds at the edge of the river Nile, or on vellum, which was made from animal pelts. But the most common **writing** material was a pointed stick called a stylus, which was used to write in the surface of a wax sheet kept in a wooden case, or tablet. Then, when the page was full, the wax could be scraped flat to start again.

Alexandria was the largest city in Roman Egypt and had been a huge port and civic centre for hundreds of years before the Romans came to Egypt. It was named after Alexander the Great, who was buried there, and as well as being home to the sadly destroyed great library, it also housed the Pharos, a giant lighthouse that was one of the seven wonders of the world.

Fortuna was one of many Roman gods and goddesses. The Romans had a god for almost everything. If the crops failed, Ceres the goddess of crops was angry. If you won a great battle, Mars the god of war was happy. Fortuna was the goddess of luck and she was worshipped all over the Roman world in many forms.

CPSIA information can be obtained at www.ICGtesting.com
Printed in the USA
LVOW11s0330130816

500214LV00005B/211/P